WHY ARE WE IN VIETNAM?

BOOKS BY NORMAN MAILER

The Naked and the Dead
Barbary Shore
The Deer Park
Advertisements for Myself
Deaths for the Ladies (and Other Disasters)
The Presidential Papers
An American Dream
Cannibals and Christians
Why Are We in Vietnam?
The Deer Park—A Play
The Armies of the Night
Miami and the Siege of Chicago
Of a Fire on the Moon
The Prisoner of Sex
Maidstone
Existential Errands
Marilyn
The Faith of Graffiti
The Fight
Genius and Lust
The Executioner's Song
Of Women and Their Elegance

NORMAN MAILER

WHY ARE WE IN VIETNAM?

A Novel

An Owl Book

Holt, Rinehart and Winston
New York

Library of Congress Cataloging in Publication Data
Mailer, Norman.
Why are we in Vietnam?
"An Owl book."
I. Title.
PS3525.A4152W47   1982   813'52   81–7261
ISBN 0–03–059977–6 (pbk.)   AACR2

First published in hardcover by
G. P. Putnam's Sons in 1967.

First Owl Book Edition—1982

Printed in the United States of America
1 3 5 7 9 10 8 6 4 2

ISBN 0-03-059977-6

TO MY FRIENDS

Roger Donoghue
Buzz Farbar
Mickey Knox
Norman Podhoretz
Cy Rembar
and
Jose Torres

PREFACE

This is the only novel I ever finished under the mistaken belief I was writing not this kind of novel but another. Living in Provincetown on the edge of those rare, towering and windy dunes which give the tip of Cape Cod a fair resemblance to the desert of the Sahara, I had begun to think of a novel so odd and so horrible that I hesitated for years to begin it. I did not like the story; it came to me with fear. I imagined a group of seven or eight bikers, hippies and studs plus a girl or two living in the scrub thickets which sat in some of the valleys between the dunes. Only six feet high, those thickets were nonetheless forests, and if one could find a path through the thorns and cat briars, nobody could track you, not in a hurry. So I peopled the thickets with characters: my characters were as wild as anyone who ever came to Provincetown. It is not a tame place. Years ago, a First Lady was once told it was "the Wild West of the East," and that is not a bad description. The tip of Cape Cod curls in on itself in a spiral—the long line of the dunes comes around like the curve of one's palm and fingers as they close into a fist—it is one of the very few places in America where one comes to the end of the road for a more profound reason than real estate ceasing to be profitable. In Provincetown, geography runs out, and you are surrounded by the sea.

So it is a strange place. The Pilgrims landed there before they went on to Plymouth—America began here. The Pilgrims lost interest in scrub pine, mournful winds, and sand in the land. They moved on, left ghosts. Whaling captains settled in later, left ghosts. In winter the town is filled with spirits. One can go mad in that rainy climate waiting for March to end. It is a place for murderers and suicides. If decades went by without a single recorded homicide, that record ended abruptly with a crime of true carnage. A few years ago, a young Portuguese from a family of fishermen killed four girls, dismembered their bodies, and buried the pieces in twenty small and scattered graves.

That catastrophe was not a good deal worse than anything I had already contemplated for my gang, since I conceived of them making nocturnal trips from the dunes into town where out of the sheer boredom of an existence not nearly intense enough to satisfy their health, they would commit murders of massive brutality and then slip back to the dunes. Motiveless crimes. I saw a string of such crimes.

I was, as I say, in fear of the book. I loved Provincetown and did not think that was a good way to write about it. The town is so naturally spooky in mid-winter and provides such a sense of omens waiting to be magnetized into lines of force that the novel in my mind seemed more a magical object than a fiction, a black magic.

Nonetheless, I began the book in the spring of '66. It attracted me too much not to begin. Yet because I could not thrust Provincetown into such literary horrors without preparation, I thought I would start with a chapter about hunting bear in Alaska. A prelude. I would have two tough rich boys, each as separated from social convention as any two rich boys could be—Texans I would make them out of a reserve of memories of Texans I had served with in the 112th Cavalry out of San Antonio. The boys would be still young, still mean rather than uncontrollably murderous—the hunting might serve as a bridge to get them ready for more. They would come back from the Alaskan hunting trip ready to travel—Provincetown would eventually receive them.

Now, anyone who reads the book which follows this preface will see that nobody ever gets to Provincetown. The chapter on hunting becomes a half-dozen chapters, a dozen chapters, it ends up being all of the book. If I wrote those chapters wondering how long it would take to extricate myself with novelistic integrity from all the elaborations of the hunt I seemed more and more bound to get into, it was not until those boys were back in Dallas and I was getting ready to move them East that I realized two things.

(1) I had nothing further to say about them.

(2) Even if I did, I could no longer believe that Tex and D.J. could still be characters in the Provincetown novel. They had another quality by now.

So I lived with my manuscript for a few months and ended by recognizing that I hadn't been too bright. I had written a novel not a prelude. The book was done. Later, a number of readers would think *Why Are We In Vietnam?* was far and away my best book. I thought I had never written a funnier book.

In retrospect, I was less certain, however, of the humor. For when Sharon Tate was murdered in the summer of '69, and the world heard of Charles Manson, I could wonder what state of guilt I might have been in if I had

3

written that novel of desert murderers. How then could I ever have been certain Manson had not been sensitive to its message in the tribal air.

But then writing has its own occult force. At its best, we never know where our writing comes from nor who gives it to us. If Jack Kennedy's name is invoked in the first sentence of *An American Dream,* nine lines farther down that page, a man named Kelly is mentioned. Later in the same Chapter we learn Kelly's middle name is Oswald—Barney Oswald Kelly. That chapter appeared in *Esquire* about a month after the assassination, but it had been written three months earlier, a coincidence to force one to contemplate the very design of coincidence.

So, too, had I written in *Barbary Shore* about a secret agent named McLeod who had been, in his time, a particularly important Soviet agent. He lived in a cheap room on the top floor of a cheap rooming house just across the hall from the narrator. Writing the book, I always found it hard to believe that such a man would be found in such a place, and that simple difficulty of not quite believing what I wrote did not help to speed the writing of the book. A year after it was published, I rented a room in a dank old building with high ceilings called Ovington Studios on Fulton Street in Brooklyn not a half mile from the rooming house in *Barbary Shore,* and on the floor below during those ten years I kept the studio was Colonel Rudolph Abel, the most important Soviet spy in America—or, at least, so was he described by the FBI when the arrest was finally made.

We will never know if primitive artists painted their caves to show a representation, or whether the moving hand was looking to placate the forces above and the forces below. Sometimes, I think the novelist fashions a totem

4

just as much as an aesthetic, and his real aim, not even known necessarily to himself, is to create a diversion in the fields of dread, a sanctuary in some of the arenas of magic. The flaws of his work can even be a part of his magical strength, as if his real intent in writing is to alter the determinations of that invisible finger which has written and moved on. By such logic, the book before you is a totem, not empty of amulets for the author against curses, static, and the pervasive malignity of our electronic air.

★

———————
———————

INTRO BEEP 1

———————
———————

★

Hip hole and hupmobile, Braunschweiger, you didn't invite Geiger and his counter for nothing, here is D.J. the friendLee voice at your service—hold tight young America—introductions come. Let go of my dong, Shakespeare, I have gone too long, it is too late to tell my tale, may Batman tell it, let him declare there's blood on my dick and D.J. Dicktor Doc Dick and Jek has got the bloods, and has done animal murder, [out out damn fart] and murder of the soldierest sort, cold was my hand and hot.

7

Braunschweiger = Smoked liver
                         Sausage
Lee = confederate general-served in Texas 1855-
                                                    61

Well, now, friends and lovers, that means you out there in all that implosion land, dig into this—*no such thing as a totally false perception.* Have you ever contemplate? Listen, dig, Edison says—quote this from McLuhan—*"I start with the intention to increase the speed of the Atlantic Cable, but when I've arrived part way in my straight line I meet with a phenomenon, and it leads me off in another direction and develops into a phonograph."* And that's how Miles Davis was born. Bangalore, don't snore—here's the bulge: Edison was hip, baby, the way you make it is on the distractions. Leave a little of your shit behind each time, that's charity for all. There is probably no such thing as a totally false perception. Por ejemplo, I say Christ is in this toothpaste tube. Duba doo, duba duba doo—there has to be some grain of true. By gum, man, bite on D.J.'s Texas dick—America, this is your own wandering troubadour brought right up to date, here to sell America its new handbook on how to live, how to live in this Electrox Edison world, all programmed out, Prononzo! (this last being the name King Alonso gave to the Spanish royal condom.) Well, Huckleberry Finn is here to set you straight, and his asshole ain't itching, right? so listen to my words, One World, it's here for adolescents and overthirties—you'll know what it's all about when you and me are done, like the asshole belonged to Egypt, man, and the penis was the slave of the Hebes and the Brews, for they got it girdled with a ring of blood fire, and the nose was the

8

Negroes, for they split it. Now, remember! Think of cunt and ass—so it's all clear. We're going to tell you what it's all about. Go go, Dr. Jek tell the folk, we're here to rock, the world is going shazam, hahray, harout, fart in my toot, air we breathe is the prez, present dent, and God has always wanted more from man than man has wished to give him. Zig a zig a zig. That is why we live in dread of God. Make me another invention, Edison. Bring in the electric come machine. Do you know I think there's a tape recorder in heaven for each one of us? and all the while we're sleeping and talking and doing our daily acts, bonging the gong, blasting the ass, chewing the milch, milking the chintz, and working the jerk, why there is that tape recorder taking it all down, this is D.J. broadcasting from Texas, from Dallas, Big D in Tex, and listen children to your old dear ma, ever notice how blood smell like cunt and ass all mix in one, but rotten, man, the flesh all rotten like meat and fish is biting each other to death, and Death where is your gates, Mother Fucker, are they hot? Big ass tomb, big ass tomb, the fish are in the fireplace and the nerve's begun to sing, make it cool, D.J., make it cool.

CHAP ONE

Well, now," said Mrs. Jethroe, the mother of this extraordinary late adolescent on the fast receding previous page, the one who calls himself D.J. (if you recalled) "well, now," said she, "what am I going to do with Ranald? He's as obscene as a barmaid and just as barmy. The boy needs to be spanked. I would just as soon spank a puma. He's evil," said Mrs. Jethroe to her psychiatrist, who is a Jewish fellow, nothing other, working his ass off in Dallas, which means so to speak that he must spend eight to ten clammy periods of fifty

minutes each listening to Dallas matrons complain
about the sexual habits of their husbands, all ex hot
rodders, hunters, cattlemen, oil riggers, corporation
gears and insurance finks, zap! Well, like every one of
these bastards (as Mrs. Jeth—call her Death-row Jethroe
—might say when her breath is big! like the bottom of
a burnt-out bourbon barrel) well, every one of these
bastards has the sexual peculiarities of red-blooded
men, which is to say that one of them can't come unless
he's squinting down a gunsight, and the other won't
produce unless his wife sticks a pistol up his ass—that
man is of course a cop. If the psychiatrist wasn't such
a fink and such a nice Jewish fellow type as to be working for the general good and wheel of society, and if
he wasn't afraid of drilling a little career-and-cancer
piss right into the heart of Texas, he would write this
book about the ejaculatory jump habits of cops, big
ass Southern redneck cops all bullwhipped and bull-
shitted up into putteez, son, they come more ways—I
froth at the mouth, said the killer, but don't think it's
spit. Well, what's to say, D.J.'s mother, Death-row
Jethroe, is the prettiest little blonde you ever saw
(looks like a draw between young Katherine Anne
Porter and young Clare Boothe Luce, whew) all perfume snatchy poo, appears thirty-five, is forty-five, airs,
humors, curl to her mouth, half Texas ass accent, half
London wickedness, trill and thrill, she's been traveling around the world, Heartache House in Bombay
and Freedom House in Bringthatpore, shit, she's been

12

getting cunt-tickled and fucked by all the Class I Dongs
in Paris and London, not to mention the upper dedi-
cated pricks of Rome and Italy while her hus, big
daddy Rusty Jethroe, is keeping up the corporation
end all over the world including Dallas, Big D, Tex.
That's some end, son, Big N we call it. Mum's first
name is Alice. They found her vagina in North Caro-
lina and part of her gashole in hometown Big D. Why?
Why was her parts metaphorically blasted? Because,
man, she used a dynamite stick for a phallus. You try
that sometime for lots of hymen. D.J.'s father, Big
Daddy, old Rusty, has got the dynamite. He don't
come, he explodes, he's a geyser of love, hot piss, shit,
corporation pus, hate, and heart, baby, he blasts, he's
Texas willpower, hey yay!

Does this idyll of family life whet your curiosity,
flame your balls, or sour your spit? Don't argue, Alice
Hallie Lee Jethroe is speaking to her Doc, Clam Fink,
the Texas Jew, actually his name is Leonard Levin
Fichte Rothenberg, pronounced by all big mind
Texans as Linnit Live'n Fixit Rottenbug.

"Well, now Lionhard," says Hallelujah Death-row,
D.J.'s sweet blond mother to Dr. Fixit, that little ole
rottenbug, "will you jes take a fix on what dear Ranald
has to say about everything? It's enough to make a
mother wipe up Aunt Jemima's puke. For I love him
like a jewel even if he is a thief. But he's out of his
mind. Poor sad little fellow. He's so delicate and beautiful even if he is barmy as a barmaid."

"Hallie, let's adjust our sense of the real," says Dr. Hebrew Hairy. "Ranald's delicacy and beauty are memory engravings, perhaps are chromosomal etchings, RNA, DNA, RNA, DNA, one for the left eye, one for the right."

"RNA, DNA, RNA, DNA," says Hallelujah.

"The facts," says Fichte, "are these: Your son, Ranald, is six feet one at the age of eighteen, and is considered highly attractive by his social compeers, as well as mean and vicious."

"He read the Marquis de Sade at the age of fifteen."

"And the drug addict William Burroughs, whom personally I can't see as a talent, I mean give me a hot pastrami sandwich, is now his hero."

"Do you mean the Hot Pastrami, Live'n Fixit?" asks Hallelujah.

"No, sir, I mean William Burroughs. Adjust your sense of the real, Alice Hallie Lee Jethroe, the time has come to program out your attitudes. I saw Ranald at your request, he was recalcitrant, charming, gracious, anti-Semitic, morally anesthetized, and smoldering with presumptive violence, a host of incense, I mean incest fixes, murder configurations, suicide sets, disembowelment diagrams and diabolism designs, mandalas! Face into the eye of the real, Hallelujah, he's a humdinger of a latent homosexual highly over-heterosexual with onanistic narcissistic and sodomistic overtones, a choir task force of libidinal cross-hybrided vectors."

"He has high-breed vectors all rights," says Hallelujah, "he's got the cunningest ancestry, in fact, cause we're on my mother's side from the Norloins."

"New Orleans?"

"Yis, from Norlins, the Norlins Frenchy Montesquious and the Bat Fartsmotherers." But seeing that Levin Fichte is living on her word, she just knocks over a bottle of one of his urine specimens, adieu albumen! and says, "Mon Doo Ginsberg, you're sure full of shit for a doctor, don't y'know there are no fine Southern families called Fartsmotherer? Lord knows we ain't that fucking stupid, why even British county stock wouldn't be called Fartsmotherer, maybe Assknocking, but not the other, you can't analyze me Living Fichte if you don't know things like that, oh poo I wish you was an Italianate Jew, all earthy and Levantine and suave and had a cunt-tickler of a mustache, instead of your clammy cold Lithuanian brow, what are you, a Talmud hokum? speak up, ass, I just wish you was good enough to kiss my sweet perfumed powdered old pootytoot, hey Linnit? am I getting out my egressions now?"

"I would not call them aggressions so much as identity crises," said Linnit.

"Oh, poo, let me tell you about the Montesquious. Half-Portuguese, half-French, all that hot crazy blood packed one-quarter into me, for the other half of mah mother was just straight Arkansas mule, the Mulies, why they the richest family in Arkansas then, hot out of Peezer, Arkansas, and they used rat paper for tar paper on the Chic Sale, that's how benighted was their latrine, army folk of course, the MacArthurs used to kiss their ass. And my daddy, well he was just a lover of a husband to my ma, and he must have had a dick on him like a derrick, do I shock you, Dr. Jew?"

"To my cornplasters."

"Oh, Linnit, you'll be the death of me yet. Listen to this old hen cackle. Well, Daddy was Indian for sure, and he had a personal odor like hot rocks in the sun which is in me all mixed with the fine sauces of Franco-Portuguese Montesquiou rut—I mean you should smell my armpits, noxious to some, a knockout to others, I keep them perfumed of course, we want no barmaid's fatal scent on Hallie Jethroe, so I wash, Dr. Rothenberg, three times a day, I don't want nothing but a soupçon of my good sweet crazy full-blooded woman's scent on the breeze off my knees, just enough for to keep the breed alive, talk of high-breed vectors, well, my own sweet husband, Big Daddy, David Rutherford Jethroe Jellicoe Jethroe, *Rusty,* is just as high breed as you want, I can't even follow Rusty's family, they're all marshals, and bastards and cowboys, and one desperado, and one railroad tycoon, and one professor at Harvard, first Texas professor they ever had in Upper Clam City, near Clamsville, which is what I call Harvard, now Linnit, you're a Harvard man, tell me straight and clear what I am going to do with Ranald, he's insane, that boy, and he looks just like George Hamilton the actor, who I think is Instant

16

Heaven, he's so brood-looking, yes, there's something
Hebrew about Ranald, he's so big and dark and mysterious for eighteen, and he goes all the way back to
Egypt you just know unlike you, dear Jew, you Talmud hokum, you clammy Have-it grit, I suppose I now
have to pony up my fifty dollars for the hour."

"Madame, you owe me eleven hundred and fifty."

"You'll have to bust a nut to get it, Rottenbug."

"I'll torture you, I love torturing gentile females.
All that white buttermilk flesh. Yum, yum. Yum, yum,
yum."

Hey, hey, they really talk that way? That little blond
lady, Hallie-perfume and powder on the poo—she talk
that way? And Rottenbug going yum yum yum—is he
out of his fucking skull? Wait and see. Nobody's got
any OK patience any more, just cannibals asking for
chocolate on their stick—how the hell do you know
what Hallie's saying to Linnit and Fixit saying back?
Wait and see? You know what they're doing. They're
talking about Tex, Tex Hyde, Gottfried "Texas"
Hyde Junior, that's D.J.'s best friend, and know what,
get that drop of cream off your jeans before you grow
hair in your hand, this is the pitch, Tex is half-German
and half-Indian on his father's side, Redskin and Nazi
all in one paternal blood, and his mother, well, bless
his mother, Tex Hyde's mother is jes old rawhide
Texas ass family running back thru fifty-two shacks
where in each shack the beans in the pot have been
stuck on blacky inside side of the pot for six weeks—

those beans look like gravel, Marshal Bean—yeah,
Tex's mother runs fifty-two shacks right back to the
Alamo where all old saddlesore real Texas ass families
run back to, why lick the scab on LBJ's knee if one-
tenth of all the Dallas ass families that go back to the
Alamo was really there, they'd have all drowned in shit
they were so congested and Santa Ana could have
thrown his marijuana seed on the top and there'd be a
forest of hemp now right in the heart of Texas. Which
is a favorite theory of the voice you hear now sub-
mitted which is that the best hash and cannabis is
grown on fertilizer of human shit, who is there to
disprove an honest man's folklore?

Well, Tex Hyde, he's a mother fucker, sell you pot
was grown on human shit, and he nothing but D.J.'s
best friend. And they are terrible together. Listen to
Halleloo. Her tone is full of hell right now, Line It
With Hot Bugs is shifting in horror in his seat, cause
Halleloo is talking in her bitchy boozy voice which
means don't come near unless you can steer your prick
like a whip and French tickler all in one, worm! us
women know which man has got the spring and who
and which is the unfortunate dead ass, here is her
words, "Tex Hyde is the son of an *undertaker*, I mean
think of that, a Montesquiou Jellicoe Jethroe a-whop-
ping around with a Kraut mortician's offspring, and all
that bastard Indian Hyde blood in the background,
firewater and dirty old Engine oil, Indians unless
they're descended from my daddy's line, and never you

mind what it was, don' ask if it's Navaho, Apache, or
any of those Jew shit questions, you anthropologist
manqué, you fuckless wonder listening to the sex'l
habits of all us mule-ass Texans, ought to get your ears
wiped out Dr. Fink Lenin Rodzianko whateva your
name is, an Indian don't tell the secret of his name in a
hurry to strangers like you, Clam Grits from Harvard
Square, why, honey, that Tex Hyde don't have Eenyen
blood like my daddy and my Rusty's daddy's daddy,
no, it's just the sort of dirty vile polluted cesspool
Eenyen blood like Mexican—you know just a touch of
that Latin slicky shit in it, vicious as they come, and
mated up, contemplez-vous, to fatty Bavarian oonshick
and poonshick jawohl furor lemme kiss your dirty
socks my leader, can you imagine? the filthiest of the
Indians and the slimiest of red hot sexyass Nazis fucking each other, mating and breeding to produce Tex
Hyde who grows up in his daddy's big booming business which is stuffing corpses and doing God knows
what to their little old pithy bowels and their dropped
stomachs and whatever else corpses got which must be
plenty or why pay thousands of dollars for a funeral
unless it's a fumigation, hey Tonto? and that boy growing up there comes out like a malevolent orchid in a
humus pile, or a black panther, that's what he is, black
panther with all his black panther piss, I'm dreaming
of him, Linnit, and so is my son, the black puma, he's
got my son who's just as beautiful as George Hamilton
and more clean-cut swearing by him, the puma and the

panther, I think they took the vow of blood, cut their thumbs and ran 'em around the rim of some debutante's pussy, after the way these kids now live there ain't much left for them but to gang fuck tastefully wouldn't you say, speak up, Linnit."

"Now, Hallie, I know you're not going to listen to me."

"But I am, my dear. I fully intend to, Linnit?"

"Yes, milady."

"Tell me I've been ladylike. I know I haven't. I know I've been outré and spouting great clouds of baloney from inner space, I mean you might think my language was the proper vocabulary for a roughneck or a driller, but I adore you, Linnit, cause you got a kind Jewish heart and I always said when Hitler killed the Jews, half the kindness went out of the world."

"Now tell me he shoulda killed the other half."

"Heh heh, heh heh. Gallows humor, Linnit."

"Hallie, are you saying you've got to separate those boys?"

"I know, I know. But they're stuck to each other like ranch dogs in a fuck. Hunting together, playing football together on the very same team, riding motorcycles together, holding hands while they ride, studying karate together, I bet they can't even get their rocks off unless they're put-putting in the same vaginal slime, I hope at least Ranald has got the taste and sentiment to be putting it in the young lady's vagina rather than going up her dirt-track where old Tex Hyde belongs (after all those bodies he helped his fat

growing rich daddy embalm, baby) but kiss the lint
from my navel, Linnit, a mother can't even be sure of
that anymore, because, *tiens, mon amour,* I even heard
of a debutante knock-up case where the boy who had to
accept the onus of parenthood was one who had ad-
dressed himself to the fore, his buddy's lawyer got him
to admit that cardinal fact by the following examination, 'Would you, Son, be so filthy and so foul as to
address yourself to a young lady's dirt track.' 'Of
course I wouldn't,' said this idiot called Son, 'do you
think I'm a pervert?' 'Well, my client is, would, and
did,' said the lawyer, 'so you are the proud papa, the
Brains rest,' end of case.

"Take the undertaker out of it," said Linnit, "that's
what disturbs your sense of peers and social compeers.
A mortician is at a social disadvantage in stable struc-
turification of society, but it's not to be calibrated on a
final scale. If Tex Hyde were the son of a normal
occupation father, for instance if Gottfried Hyde Senior was straight corporation exec like Rusty."

"No, no, no, Rottenbug, you're thinking like a tick
again."

"If the boys were the same in the back room, so to
speak, *sotto voce,*" said Lenin Fink, "in the easy come
and go, the rhodomontade—if you permit me—of
similar breedings and backings, would you then object
to the highly cathected vectors of their friendship?"

"Bless you, but I would."

"Tell me why, pie."

"Because Tex grew up a undertaker's son, fool!

plunging his hands into dead people's vitals, picking up through his fingertips all sorts of black occult steamy little grimes of things, swamp music and black lightning and soundless thunder—purple wonders, it's like sleeping the night in a rotten old stump—who knows what song the maggots sing, and what aromatic intuitions inflame the brain. Herbs are the nerve to a fearsome underworld—listen, baby, I didn't get fucked by Aleister Crowley for nothing, those passes at the Black Masses," said Hallie, putting a gloved finger up to her dear chin—she is incidentally now lying her ass off because she's too young to know Aleister Crowley, but she's like her son, D.J., she's got to brag, better believe it.

Well, this has gone on long enough. Cause you ought to know who had produced this material. Color it rainbow. This has been D.J. presenting to you the private scene of his mother being psychoanalyzed by that clammy little fink, and if the illusion has been conveyed that my mother, D.J.'s own mother, talks the way you got it here, well little readster, you're sick in your own drool, because my mother is a Southern lady, she's as elegant as an oyster with powder on its ass, she don't talk that way, she just thinks that way. Do we understand each other now, son? You've had fun long enough. The serious shit soon starts. You're contending with a genius, D.J. is his name, only American alive who could outtalk Cassius Clay, that's lip, duck the blip, Orlando, it's right on your radar screen.

★

===

INTRO BEEP 2

===

★

The fact of the matter is that you're up tight with a mystery, me, and this mystery can't be solved because I'm the center of it and I don't comprehend, not necessarily, I could be traducing myself. Por ejemplo, the simple would state that Intro Beep One is a stream-of-conch written by me, and consequently commented upon by my mother up tight with her libido-drained psychoanalyst. But now you know Chap One with Fink Razzbah (rhymes with Casbah) is made up by me, D.J., alias Ranald such-and-such such-and-such Jethroe,

Disc Jockey to the world (my mental connections are faster than anything afoot) and lightning which is a special case of light—how about that, Zack! is not proof against the rapidity of my investigations. For light is the content of a medium called lightning—Old McLuhan's going to be breaking his fingernails all over again when he hears this. So watch out for D.J., muzzfuckers. Gather here, footlings and specialists, hot shit artists, those who give head, and general drug addicts of the world, which means all you Hindus and professional football asshole buffs, and glom onto the confusion of my brain. It might be a tape recording, right? A tape recording of my brain in the deep of its mysterious unwindings. Maybe there will be a day when they discover how to dig it out, and then I will be the first living archaeological exhumation, the first documentary source of prime existence, Living Man, here he thinks, listen in, Humphrey! and then D.J. will be revered because documentaries are the bleeding-heart gods of the future out there in old electronic land. Did you ever know the seat of electricity? It's the asshole. But what then is the asshole of electricity? Why Creation, Catherine, that's what it is. I mean just think of the good Lord, *A*men, and all the while we're sleeping and talking and eating and walking and pissing and fucking, excuse me, Lord, *A*men! *A*men! why, there's that Lord, slipping right into us, making an *operation* in the bowels of Creation so there's a tiny little transistorized tape recorder not as big as a bat's gnat's nut,

24

why a million angels can dance on the idiot pinhead of that tape recorder, DNA, RNA, right? and it takes it all down, it makes all the mountainous files of the FBI look like paper cuttings in a cat-shit box, and so there is the good Lord, king of the Rat Finks, I mean, Sultan of the Wrathful Things, forgive me, Lord, yeah, yeah, there *He* is getting a total tape record of each last one of us, wow, double wow, rumble woof, beat the tweeter, Vera Elvira, everything you ever thought and your accompanying systole and diastole and pisshole and golden asshole all recorded, your divine intuitions and cloacal glut, all being put down FOREVER on a tiny piece of microfilm (or some such membraneous receptor) all of it being compressed by the Super File Compressor until the Lord wants to tune in on you and so presumes to press a Nuraloid button and all of you is transmogrified into one little beep the microfilm gives up, cause that's it with sound, infinitely compressible—with smell you can waft your ass and nose from here to the black hole of Calcutta—but every sound in a symphony is contained in the bong of one gong, just as all Creation is heard and felt in the shriek of the tight wire in one pebble piss-or-pinch orgasm—weep for all of us poltroons who have felt such woe, Broad Lightning!—and now face your consequence, the Lord hears your beep, the total of all of you, good and bad, sharp and flat, chords, disharmonies and minor twelfths —wheeze! Give up the breath—one of his angels passes you on. To here or to there. Yeah.

25

Unless you can put false material into the tape recorder. Think of that.

It opens this hypothesis. I, Ranald, S-and-S Jethroe, working as D.J., may be trying to trick Number One Above, maybe I'm putting false material into *this* tape recorder, or jamming it—contemplate! Maybe I'm making cheerful humorous recs, belly laughter shit pressings when in fact I'm sheer fucked right out of my mind, how about that? Maybe all this humor here is absolute pretense, maybe—up your buns, J. D. Salinger —I'm coming on like Holden Caulfield when I'm really Doctor Jekyll with balls. I mean I got a horror in me, honey, I will not tell you yet. I will merely offer the clue—we have no material physical site or locus for this record, because I can be in the act of writing it, recording it, slipping it (all unwitting to myself) into the transistorized electronic aisles and microfilm of the electronic Lord (who, if he is located in the asshole, must be Satan) or I can be expiring consciousness, I can be the unwinding and unravelings of a nervous constellation just now executed, killed, severed or stopped, maybe even stunned, you thunders, Herman Melville go hump Moby and wash his Dick.

Or maybe I'm a Spade and writing like a Shade. For every Spade is the Shade of the White Man, and when we die we enter their mind, we are part of the Shade. And when Spades die?—well, that depends on how you dig Niggers you white ass chiggers says D.J. Come on now, says D.J., what if I'm not the white George

Hamilton rich dear son of Dallas, Texas, and Hallelujah ass but am instead black as your hole after you eat
licorice and chew black cherries, what then, what if I'm
some genius brain up in Harlem pretending to write a
white man's fink fuck book in revenge, ever see an old
black man roll his eyes on a country road while some
ice-green-eye redneck look him in and out saying what
black thoughts you have Sambo ass, and Mr. Black he
looking back and he see Whitey the Green Eye from
Texas with his ears moving in circles like old wasp
wings, zzz, and his sharp Scotch-Irish White White
White Man's Nose red as lobster is a-hovering and a-
plunging like a Claw, man, look at the white-green
snots way up high, Niggerman, this is D.J. broadcasting from Texas, maybe, Doctor Jek out on his frants
again, sick with the tick, ex-acid is my head, Love iS
Death, HelL iS Death, it's square to be frantic, so bring
in the cool, bring in the cool, D.J., tell the folk in the
cool of the evening that they are listening to Mr. Big,
Mister Big Blood, oh blood how rot is thy sting? So you
can't know if I'm true-blue Wasp-ass Texas even if I
know and that's a fact, cause I know I'd like to walk up
to Jesus some day and shake 'is hand and look 'em in the
eye, and say Son, Y'may have lost the law suit, but have
no hard feelings and come around again soon—we miss
Y' down in this neck of the woods which ain't got much
woods, nor trees for that matter, jus mud and dust and
cattle and cow shit in abunnance, but Y're welcome,
Y're surely welcome, Y're a man's man, Y're a peach,

Y're a peach of a little whining Jew bastard, Jesus, each time I go hunting my wife won't fuck. That's Christianity for you—jes insists on using shit for axle grease in the heat of the chase.

Nonetheless, if you are really reading this and I am really writing it (which I don't know—it's a wise man who knows *he* is the one who is doing the writer's writing—we are all after all agents of Satan and the Lord, cause otherwise how explain the phenomenological extremities of hot shit and hurricane) but assuming howsomever that this huge metaphysical appropriation of the possibilities is valid that to wit that I, Dr. Jekyll, D.J. for genius, eighteen plus years old, is in fact writing this, then I better stop bullshitting the record and commit a few facts. Get set for my father in Chap Two. Release your horny masturbating hand. Engorge your lip. Take a fearsome trip.

CHAP TWO

D.J.'s father, the cream of corporation corporateness, Rutherford David Jethroe Jellicoe Jethroe, came back to Dallas after spending twelve years off and on moving around the world for Central Consolidated Chemical and Plastic, CCCP being what the boys called it till they found out the Red-ass Russians had their Communist Party initials CCCP, so they changed the name —look into the difficulties—an approval vote of the stockholders 1,178,008 to 241,642, change of listing on the stock market, reams of pure shit, reprinting of

stationery, invoices, packages, loading, relettering box-
cars—they a bunch of tight assholes running the inner
mills of the mills, so guess the new name, you know it,
they called it Central Consolidated *Combined* Chemical and Plastic, the new coagulation of title now being
CCCCP or as the team began to say, 4C and P, which is
an unhappy conjunction since how much can you fore-
see before you got—well, they say people in the Corporate life shoot their urine straighter than a '03 Spring-
field, we ain't Wasp-like for nothing, y' hear Rangoon?
So back came Rusty after twelve big years in the foreign ass vineyards setting up operations for Double CC
and Plastic, as *he* called it, his other fond name being
Central Consolidated, cause they call it that too out
where the reindeer run and the flying fishes try out
their flying CIA fucks past Mandalay, and he was
brought back in to head a new division for Four C-ing
the cancer market—big lung subsidiary. Whereas
Foreseeing Plastic wanted to get in on the bright new
fortunes being made along the rim-scab of Carcinoma
Cruds and Craters which D.J. is here to tell you is
America's Last Frontier and Marching Estate, so leave
Corporate Wisdom to its devices, they come up with a
plastic filter for cigarettes which offers more pores in it
than Sponge Valley, in fact if you perspire too much
you can tape one of these cigarette filters to your
armpit, that'll absorb the Chinese cooking and general
underarm funk; should a petting party hose-down and
gism-shoot occur, as it may with the best of young

friends and associates, why, stick our plastic filter up said girl's tootle and all misdirected gism will be absorbed, no prononzo necessary here, but never, unless you're the Earl of Roderick, try to proctate it up her ass or she will never again be able to tinkle and will die *emmerdé!!* Whang! Whang! this plastic filter—trade name Pure Pores—is the most absorptive substance devised ever in a vat—traps all the nicotine, sucks up every bit of your spit. Pure Pores also causes cancer of the lip but the surveys are inconclusive, and besides, fuck you!

Well, back came Rusty to Dallas to head Pew Rapports—the filter with the purest porosity of purpose—and Rusty was a heroic-looking figure of a Texan, 6½, 194, red-brown lean keen of color, eyes gray-green-yellow-brown which is approved executive moderate shit hue color for eyes if you want to study corporation norms mores and tempos of shift and success in massive organizational configurations, and since he was big exec, what do you think he look and talk like? Well, Clara, go to the rear of the line, he look like a high-breed crossing between Dwight D. Eisenhower and Henry Cabot Lodge, what the buns do you think a corporation exec is going to look like if he got the time to make his face grow the way he want it to grow during all the Fifties while he's overseas, I mean what face did he ever see more of than Dwight D., and Henry C. working his axe, at the UN, these corporation eggzex are full of will, man, they're strong as bulls these hide-ass Waspy mules

Henry Cabot Lodge (1850-1924)
—Senator

with their silvy rim specs, I mean they go direction
they want to go, their hair too curly they go bald, their
nose too long, they sniff it up, their lips too fat, forget
it, we're talking about the wrong man, they tie that
nice dry-oiled West Point ramrod to their back just
like they're a tomato plant on a stick, I mean they grow
into a bat's ass if it help our astronauts along, Rusty
and his ilk is hard-working. He zip that corporation fly,
dig, while working as executive, and/or director,
and/or special adviser and/or consultant and/or
troubleshooter and/or organizer and/or associate of,
and/or paid employee for the 4C and P, the CIA, the C
of C, the FBI, the ADA (yeah, he gives contribs there
too right under the table—Rusty Jethroe and Letter-
head America are Up Tight) the Policemen's Benevolent Society, the John Birch, natch, the Dallas Citizens
Council for Infighting and Inflicting Symphonic
Music, the Benevolent Order of Oilwell Riggers
Drillers and Roughnecks, the Warren Commission
Boosters, the President's Thousand Dollar Club, the
Gridiron Club, the UIA and 4A of D, that is the
Underwriters, Insurance Agents and Actuarial Agents
Association of America and Dallas, the NYSE (that's
Stock Exchange, Skeezix) the Anti-Defamation League
of the B'nai Brith, a passing honor they gave him,
totally honorary, believe you, the RELM Cons—the
Rotary, Elks, Lambs, Masons Consolidated for corpo-
ration studs who jes ain't got the time to spread out so
they put it all in one dead fuck building—and the

32

Republican Party, not to mention the Second Congre-
gated Anglo Episcopal and Conjoint Presbyterian
Clutch and Methodist Church of Maltby Avenue,
Dallas (that's St. Martin's, you faggot!) and the Gour-
met Wine and Pâté Plate and Fork Society. Forget the
country clubs unless you like to read lists, the Dallas
Elm and Tree Club, the Dallas Cowboy Turtle Creek
Cheering and Chowder, TCU Boosters, SMU
Boosters, the Gala Ring and Ranch, Eddie Bonetti's
Country Club, take it from D.J., forget this shit. If
Rusty was to run around all year, which he does, he
still couldn't get his dick in every door for which he's
got a card, you know, even Diners Club, Carte
Blanche, American Express, Rusty's a pig! he's a real
pig, man! It was all that dried-out sunbaked smoked
jerkin of meat his cowboy fore-ass bears used to eat, I
mean, man, they used to use that hide for everything
before they'd eat it, they'd swab out their mare's dock
with it, wipe their own ass with it, pick up the pus
from the corner of their eye, blow their nose, mop the
piss off their boots, even use that dry old piece of meat
to wrap around their dick for stuffing when they want
to sodomize a real big fat slack cow, why they repaired
holes in their chaps with it, they used to have to beat it
with a hoe handle before they could even cook it and
fry it in axle grease. I mean, man they were kind of
tough. No Frenchy Montesquious them. Crazy as
wolves. All greeneyed pricks. So, no wonder Rusty's a
pig. His cells are filled with the biological inheritance

and trait transmissions of his ancestors, all such raw-hide, cactus hearts, eagle eggs, and coyote. Now, Rusty rolls that Château Lafite-Mouton-Rothschild around his liver loving lips, and he can tell 49 from 53 from 59, all the while thinking of 69. He sings the song of the swine, D.J.'s daddy, nice fellow actually. Also forgot to mention he's an unlisted agent for Luce Publications, American Airlines Overseas Division, and the IIR—the Institute for International Research—shit!, Spy Heaven they ought to call it.

Eh bien, you may now inquire, be you reader, Good Lord, or the angel who's passing on this message from my asshole transistor to God, whyfor does Doctor Jekyll have such a total rejection of all the positive elements in his rich secure successful environmental scene including social backing, strong sentiment, national roots, loci of power, happy physical endowment (wait till you hear more about that) and clearly individualistic and highly articulated parents?

And D.J. says in answer: ever read *The Concept of Dread* by Fyodor Kierkegaard? No, well neither has D.J. but now he wants to know how many of you assholes even knew, forgive me, Good Lord, that Fyodor Kierkegaard has a real name, *Sören* Kierkegaard. Contemplate *that*. You ass.

Anyway, D.J. is up tight with the concept of dread. He don't have to read S.K. S.K. can stick dread up his own ass. The time is near, man. D.J. has ideas like nobody else. He sees through to the stinking roots of things, contemplate Eternity the poets might say, take a mind picture, D.J. can watch his own ass being created on Time Recaptured TV Time, eye on Big Daddy's back while he stinging D.J.'s ma, D.J. a #1 ghost on the #1 spermatozoa. Think of that. Maybe that's how Herr Dread gets in. Cause D.J. has seen his father while D.J. up high on pot, and face of Rusty goes thru chord changes then. Strange sounds, man. Neo-occult chromatics. Crowns and diadems. An octave of farts. Hurtlings, hard-edge work, cockroach scamperings, caterwaulings, rivers of cream—oh, Mary, forget it, D.J. is putting you on, that's LSD shit and William Burroughs in horse land, not sweet old tea. No, via grass, man, D.J. has seen Rusty as follows: (1) the smiling Ike grin goes away, and so do all those Henry Cabot Lodge grins, instead there's a thin lippy old hole cut for his mouth—like the first slit on an operation—skin peels back, and in the wound there's teeth—D.J. happens to know those teeth are real, cause his daddy bit him once five years ago—that's a tale! (Can you wait for your next Intro Beep?)—but those teeth look like ten grand worth of superaesthetic dentures. And his nose takes a metamorphosis or two out of the Onassis Aristotle Bank of Ideal Forms. Well, now Rusty's got normally some kind of big pointy nose with fleshy backing, good shape, but it's a tool, man. On pot, it looks suddenly like a hand, got a red mean finger at the tip, stab you right in the middle of your lie, or grab your mouth and twist it off. It's a shit

converter of a nose—any flunky talking to Rusty and
not knowing what to say cause he's hiding some fuckup
is going to find all that hardpan constipated Texas clay
in his flunky gut turning abruptly to sulfur water and
steam. Not to mention specks of zipping around deep-
sea shit. Of course, if the flunky farts in his panic,
forget it, Rusty can't bear the sight of a man who ever
broke under pressure. But it's Rusty's eyes kick off the
old concept of dread in D.J. Fyodor Sören Kierkegaard
Jethroe because they remind him of his favorite theory which is that America is run by a mysterious
hidden mastermind, a secret creature who's got a
plastic asshole installed in his brain whereby he can
shit out all his corporate management of thoughts. I
mean that's what you get when you look into Rusty's
eyes. You get voids, man, and gleams of yellow fire—
the woods is burning somewhere in his gray matter—
and then there's marble aisles, better believe it, fifty
thousand fucking miles of marble floor down those
eyes, and you got to walk over that to get to The Man,
which is only the way his eyes look to D.J. when on pot,
cause you know in a photograph or just shaking his
hand, Rusty's eyes are okay, sort of dead ass and dull
with a friendly twinkle—typical American eyes—and
when he's turned on, like when he's ready to prong a
passing cunt in a hurry—which D.J. estimates is six
eight times a year—or when he's about to consummate
the big signing (listen to the silent bagpipes) in some
ten-month pass-the-buck or stand-and-fuck game of

medium vs.
high grade
asshole

negotiations, why then Rusty's eyes are like yellow coals, liquid yellow fire ready to explode in its own success. Horses away! Polo mallets up, Bostwick! if D.J. wouldn't take to pot at family dinners he might not have such a Fyodor Kierk kind of dread looking into Big Daddy's chasm and tomb. But that dread's out there, man. Because Rusty is also the highest grade of asshole made in America and so suggests D.J.'s future: success will stimulate you to suffocate! Yeah, if they any higher grade asshole in America than Rusty why they got something on the ball comparable to life stuff, cosmological matter, Zen archery, hot shit satori, Highways and Byways of LSD, or plain hardpan thriftily won, modestly assumed, holy acquired plain old Christian Grace and Get-up, Go, Spunk. Now, they ain't that many in America. D.J. despite time overseas will not presume to assert authority in these matters for foreign lands, but in America the most stable and dependable human product we turn out, and our schools, businesses, armed forces, and legislative halls are proud to be so filled with the product, is a medium-to high-grade asshole like Rusty, who in turn obeys the orders only of G.P.A.—who, in case you forget, is Mr. Great Plastic Asshole. So don't be too hard on Rusty. He's a pig with a wild snouty mouth, but he's got good blood.

Okey-doke, Henry. The thing to understand is that a high-grade asshole is characterized by a specific and even unique property which endows him because of it with his rank—it is that a high grade of A.H. is not easily recognized as any kind of A.H., and usually appears the contrary. Despite the cock and bunghole details D.J. has furnished you up to here on some few of Rusty's opinions and habits, the portrait has been highly unfair to high-grade assholes because it has emphasized the hole rather than the high grade. Therefore, attention America to how Rusty shapes up in a contest against a man who is not an asshole—to wit, Mr. Luke Fellinka, head guide and hunter extraordinaire for the Moe Henry and Obungekat Safari Group on a hunting trip up in Brooks Range, north of Arctic Circle, Alaska. Yeah, follow along on this. Get your head clear. Get ready. Followers of D.J. are going to be hung on Alaska for a lot of high-grade genius rating consciousness now, because Rusty is the most competitive prick there is, and Big Luke is a sweet old bastard, who's so tough that old grizzly bears come up and kiss his ass. Yeah.

★

INTRO BEEP 3

★

Yeah, Rusty's a competitive prick, you know, he played for TCU, third All-American AP 1936, 1937, like back in there! look it up! and he was showing D.J. something few years ago on the back lawn of the Dallas ass mansion we inhabit, father and son—details on request, pen pal!—and he demonstrated to me I could not run around him. Well, of course D.J. did just that for a while, he ran the fucking ass off and around Rusty cause D.J. at thirteen had a presumptive hip dip halfback's butt about as big as Scarlett O'Hara's waist and

39

he could use it like a double pin universal swivel, and
Rusty had acquired a considerable amount of dead ass
sticking his brave plunger up all blindly into the cunt-
refined wickedness of Hallelujah's sophisticated rumps
and vaginal radar rays masers and lasers. I mean, he
was like the charge of the Light Brigade, not so light,
and she was one with all those houris and Fakirs and
Cossacks and Turks up in the hills who wait to pick
each zippy point of meat-nip and therefore know where
to cut on down on the Light Brigade and cut off a piece
of that charge for themselves. O Kuklos, great god of
the seasons, bring back the fox trot, cause D.J.'s em-
barrassed to tell what's next, how, he, thirteen-year-old
swivel ass flunkout in classics at the time, was running
Third Team All-America TCU tackle Rusty Death-
row's middle-aged dead ass into the Dallas lawn fertilizer when D.J. made a fatal misestimate of reckoning—
he felt sorry for his dad. He let him tackle him just
once. Jes once—right in the dry linty Dallas old navel
of Texas. Rusty was so het up, he *flung* D.J. and—mail
in your protests—he bit him in the ass, right through
his pants, that's how insane he was with frustration,
that's how much red blood was in *his* neck, and man,
he hung on, he nearly lifted D.J. up in the air with his
deathly teeth—he would have if he hadn't been a
deacon at St. Martin's. That poor D.J. He was a one-
cheek swivel ass running on one leg for the next ten
minutes while Rusty tackled him whoong! whoong!
over and over again. Trails of glory came out of his

head each time he got hit. "Randy," said Rusty, afterward, "you got to be a nut about competition. That's the way. You got to be so dominated by a desire to win that if you was to squat down on the line and there facing you was Jesus Christ, you would just tip your head once and say, 'J.C., I have to give you fair warning that I'm here to do my best to go right through your hole.'" Actually, if Rusty had ever seen J.C. on the line he'd have shit, he'd have said with a little funky wink, "Are we going to be so fortunate as to get you for the Contemporary Speaker's Series at Southern Methodist?" no, D.J.'s here to say that Rusty bit his ass so bad because he was too chicken to bite Hallelujah's beautiful butt—she'd have made him pay a half million dollars for each separate hole in her marble palace. D.J., as you may have divined, is a manly clean-featured version in formal features of his mother, and don't look like a puma or a George Hamilton at all, light brown hair, green eyes, he's just good-looking, that's all. And he was a son of sufficiently decent comportment to follow his daddy's advice. So soon as the fucking game was over (can you imagine the two of them on the back lawn of that Dallas manse?) why D.J. just limped broke-ass to the gardener's shed, picked up a pick-axe handle, and bopped his daddy over the dead center of his head, blood still running down from that bite. When Rusty didn't fall and in fact an electric shock traveled from his head down the pick-axe handle into D.J.'s overheated heart, why our boy knew in some competitions sanity was better than being a nut, so he split, man, he took off on one leg and a wound in cheek of his ass, and it took a week of negotiations by his ma to bring him out of the hideout in Mineral Wells where she'd stashed him and into audience with his father again. Who, of course, sent him to military school out in the general vicinity of McQueeney, Texas. "If it was good enough for Pres. Eisenhower, it's good enough for you," well, that was a comic book military school, all Nazi-type Texas-style state trooper wolf bugger faggots and little languid queer types from Norlins. There was even a Frenchy Montesquiou. En passant, D.J. tied a couple of pricks into pretzels and made his escape, and could if so choosing have given Linnit Fixit material for his unwritten book on the grope habits of the Southwest.

Now, of course, Rusty Jethroe ain't an habitual asshole with anyone but his son. In fact, it was an excess of love which produced such a high focus and over the threshold area of hate as those cuspy little marks on D.J.'s one of two buns which D.J. now incidentally explains to those Dallas debutantes and just plain common fucks who are lucky enough to get drilled by him and Tex, as the circular cornada produced by the slivers of a horn shattered on a fighting bull which he had engaged in a tienta south of Guadalajara, Mexico, and what's the pity, he tells the girls, is that he might have been able to distinguish himself if it hadn't been for the fact that the bull was hurt sufficiently to be withdrawn from the fucking ring while they played the Virgin of the Macaroon—that's how *dumb* those young Texas cunts can be, better believe it—and all the poor Mexican wetbacks sitting in the stands threw cascades of hot piss at him from their empty paper cups used originally for beer (in one spout, out the other) and D.J. would lick his lips, and look the sweet little Dallas cunt in the eye, and say, "Honey, that piss smelled just like your sweet little home-cooking crotch before you git up in the morning to swab it down," and your Disc Jockey here to tell that would start a real fight in the back seat of the car with D.J. his pants half-mast and laughing his ass off, and the girl developing muscles like cables made of guitar strings, they would have like to garrote him— the smell of her pussy is sacrosanct to a young girl! Mexican hot piss! Why even a little-headed, thin- nosed, big-jawed, six-foot Dallas girl would have imagi- nation enough to know what Mexican hot piss would smell like from the Rio Grande all the way to the floodlands of Anchorage, Alaska. Or even beyond to the hunting cabin.

Thus, D.J. your hot hustling guide has by native wit brought you back to the confrontation between Rusty and Big Luke the Paragon Fellinka and Ollie Totem Head Water Beaver, and their guide assistants, and the various minions and flunkies and Tex and D.J. Nose to nose soon will be Luke and Rusty. Hold on.

CHAP THREE

★

Now Rusty was supposed to go originally on Alaska safari with his opposite number Al Percy Cunningham, the managing director of Tendonex, which is 4C and P's answer to Fiberglas. Rusty and Al Percy C. had reserved an Alaska guide eighteen months in advance, you know the type that is a guide for Charley Wilson or Roger Blough or J. Edgar—I mean, that's who you got to be if you want to get this guide right away, like he wouldn't even take Senators, and you was a Congressman and you wanted Big Luke Fellinka and his assistant Ollie the Indian Water Beaver, forget it, you could lie down on your back and say Big Luke if you consent to be my guide you or Ollie can take one big crap in my mouth just for openers, and Big Luke would yawn. D.J. and Tex read right away the #1 reason all the minions of the Great Plastic Asshole were slobbering over the bear grease on Big Luke's boots. It wasn't just because among Alaska guides he was primus inter pares (you have just had the first and last of D.J.'s Latin) it wasn't cause he got eight clients out of the Brooks Mountains once in a record September blizzard, or fought a grizzly or two bare hand to a kind of draw and had the scars to show it (looked like vines and thorns had grown over an old seam of welding on his back) it wasn't even his rifle work which in offhand shooting could put in 25 one-inch five-shot clusters at 100 yards, and at two hundred yards in a half-ass clearing of woods could now and then drop a bullet into the eye of an Alaska wolf as directly as you could drop your finger in your own eye—no, what made Big Luke The Man was that he was like the President of General Motors or General Electric, pick one, I don't give a fuck, he had like the same bottom, man, I mean D.J.'s here to tell you that if you even a high-grade asshole and had naught but a smidgeon of flunky in you it would still start—you may purchase this in full confidence—it would still start in Big Luke's presence to blow sulfur water, steam, and specks of hopeless diarrhetic matter in your runny little gut,

46

cause he was a (man!) You could hang him, and he'd weigh just as much as Charley Wilson or Robert Bonehead McNamara, I mean you'd get the same intensity of death ray off his dying as you'd get from some fucking Arab sheik who had ten thousand howlers on horses to whoop and scream for the holy hot hour of his departure to Allah. So you can see what a hoedown of a hunting trip it would have been if Al Percy C. alias Kid Tendonex and Rusty had each been burning up that Alaska Brooks Mountain Range brush trying to light a light of love in Big Luke's eye, but Al Percy Cunningham was called off at the last by the Astronaut Program hotline into 4C and P because the real hoedown just that week of departure was between Fiberglas and Tendonex to see who was going to get the contract to put a plastic Univar valve and plug into the bottom of the collapsible built-in space suit chemical toilet in the Gemini (Roman Numeral Unstated) which contract is no superhuge kettle of lobster shit in volume dollars, but just a reasonable 58 million, although Tex and D.J. agree that little Univar plug is First Priority, cause let it malfunction and those astronauts will be swimming in orbits of dehydrated processed food shit (their own—a gritty performance, eh Maurice?) . However, it's edge. Does 4C and P, Tendonex Division, or FCA (Fiberglas Corp. of America) get to be the first to fling their product into space; besides there's rumors, Rusty tells us, that smooth plastic in outer space tends to exhibit Independent, Auton-

omous, Non-pattern-directed Ductile-type Magnification and Expansion Assertions in Non-Operational
Gravitational Ultra-Multi-Mach Ellipsoid Program-
Oriented Satellite Capsule Negotiations, which is to say
that smooth plastic is growing plastic hairs on its palm
while in such jerk off orbit. A big sweat is on. Whose
research program has anticipated any of this? "Cunny's
sweating this week," Rusty tells the boys. "I told him
to load up with Pure Pores once his balls started to get
wet, and he just gave me a sick little hunky hunk heh-
heh. Probably wanted to haul off and split your dad
with an axe."

But Rusty, au fond, is deeply in disappointment, not
cause A. P. Cunningham ain't with him, but because
the hunting trip is now downgraded. D.J.'s here to tell
you that in secret Rusty feels like a movie star who's
going out to pump for a weekend with the best new
Pumper-head Penis in Cinemaville, and then hears
she's missing the opportunity to have a commissary
lunch with Prince Philip or Baldy Khrushchev, before
Baldy was an ex. Well, you know a movie star, she'd
rather have Big K stomp his big shoe jes once in the
crack of her ass while he's still Mr. Big than have her
cunt stick-tickled into heaven for three days with no
one up there in the redwoods to see it except those
guests invited to the exhibition like her mother, her
father and her dramatic coach. "Hit high C next time
you come, Chérie, we got to get through those vocal
locks," says the dramatic coach.

48

Now D.J. suffers from one great American virtue, or
maybe it's a disease or ocular dysfunction—D.J. sees
right through shit. There's not a colon in captivity
which manufactures a home product that is transparency proof to Dr. Jekyll's X-ray insight. He sees
right into the claypots below the duodenum of his — 1st pt. of small intestine
father, and any son does that is fit candidate for a
maniac, right, T.S.? the point here, Eliot, is that D.J.
will never know if Rusty dropped points in the early
stages of his contest with Luke because he was dying
inside for not being down at the Canaveral table where
big power space decisions were being made by his
opposite number, Wise-Ass Cunningham, or whether
Rusty would have lost in the early stages to Big Luke
on the best week he ever had, which is an ambiguity
right at the center of D.J.'s message center. But pro-
ceed to study the scene.

Give Rusty his straight shot. If Big Al Percy Wise-
Ass Cunningham had been there, the set of events
would have had to be different. Take away A. P. Cun
and what you got—ego status embroilments between
numbers, guides and executives. All right—look into
it. You may never get out.

First, Rusty spends no time trying to be the equal of
Big Luke head on! He takes Luke's suggestions, is
friendly but aloof. When Luke addresses him as Sir, Sir
Rutherford Jet-Throne does not say call me Rusty.
When Big Luke speaks to Rusty's two accompanying
flunkies, Luke naturally picks them up by the handle

49

of their first name, and Rusty, listening, chuckles like poor Clark Gable used to when he was near the end, that is indulgently and wisely, could be worse, man, cause the two flunkies—call them Medium Asshole Pete and Medium Asshole Bill—M.A. Pete (Assistant to Procurement Manager, Pure Pores Filters Company Office of 4C and P) and M.A. Bill (Personnel Director for Production Manager, Pure Pores et cetera Company Office of 4C and P) laugh each of them separately and respectively like Henry Fonda and Jimmy Stewart. Maybe it should be said that they are Medium Assholes with a passing grade of C. Rusty could have done better, but kid you not, it ain't so easy. Talent ain't hanging on meathooks in corporation land, especially when you change plans and invitations at the last minute. Some Americans giving up a lot for the astronauts.

Now, with such for background on personnel, ask yourself Sherlock Onanist Holmes what were Rusty's expectations from this trip, I mean Rusty is corporation, right, that means he's a voice, man, he's a voice, got nothing unexpected ever to say, but he got to say it with quality. These corporation pricks are not there for nothing. They may be dumb and benighted, yeah, and D.J. has wasted his adolescence in their purlieus and company mansions and has eaten off their expense accounts all his days, D.J. knows them asshole to appetite, and can tell you, Horace, they are not all that dumb. Being medium-grade and high-grade asshole, they have high competence in tunnels and channels. They can all swim uphill through shit face first although in fact corporate faces are never seen to move, for they know enough not to try to read each other's corporate fish features when they can read each other's corporate ass voices. Man, they pick up what you're trying to slip by them, they buy nothing that's not tested, not voice-tested. So look at Rusty's problem. He goes on a Class A hunting trip—a Charley Wilson, John Glenn, Arnold Palmer, Gary Cooper kind of trip, next thing in top category you might say to a Jackie Kennedy Bobby Kennedy Ethel and the kids trip— Rusty's stepping up out of category, reaching just a bit, but if he makes out, if he comes back and is able to say, "Well, it was not a record honey-grizzly by any means, it didn't weigh out at more than twelve hundred, but Big Luke thought I got off a fair shot, and was, truth to tell, impressed with the coincidence that George Humphrey dropped one in the same glen just five years ago."

Now, pick up on the potential pitfalls. If Rusty is bird-turding he's got a lot of cabbage verbiage for which he can be faulted on. Take: fair shot. That could mean great shot; could mean piss-ass shot. George Humphrey's name equal to Pope Pius in certain executive Dallas ass chambers; therefore it's got to be dropped like a feather on velvet. Honey-grizzly has to be enunciated as if you was up tight enough with that variety of bear to tweak his nuts. So on. Mark this, fellow Americans, and file it 2R—Ready Reference—each time Rusty runs into mood-gearings of attention back home in the office, he is going to have to turn to M.A. Pete or M.A. Bill and say, "Isn't that so, Pete? isn't that so, Bill?" and they're going to have to say, "It sure is, Rusty," and say it without a trace of strain, they're yes-men, it is expected of them to be dauntless in their gut yes as they go through the yes ass gears, but perfection breeds perfection, the critical ear gets as sharp as a mad-dragster maniac-type genius listening to two 427 cubic inchers put in tandem—their yes has to have perfection precisioned. Well, even with professional bullshit, and that's the secret of the corporation—it is filled with men who are professional bullshit packers—there is a limit. A yes-man will strain his gut to produce—they are the unsung heroes of America (reason they're unsung is they can't get their tongue out of the boss' ass long enough to sing) but strain a gut as they may they cannot strain it past its own true natural elasticity. Something bona fide has got to happen, they can't just go up to Alaska woods, get drunk for a week, buy a bear skin in Fairbanks or McGrath, take pictures, and slip a suppository up the folks back home, those Texas ears too sharp. There'd be a soupçon of caviar shit in the voice and that would put a rick-tick-tick in the narrator's disc. So Rusty's got to produce something big enough for his boys, M.A. 1 and M.A. 2, to say you're right, Rusty, with an easy harmonious concordium of voice, a choir of Texas asspurring where the yeah boss you go right ahead and kick my Nigger ass gets a Texas hum. For then corporate power is cooking in Rusty's veins.

So Rusty's problem is simple. He can't begin to consider how to go back without a bear. He got a corporation mind. He don't believe in nature; he puts his trust and distrust in man. 5% trust, 295% distrust. He figures if Big Luke wants him to tag a bear, that's the ball game—if Big Luke don't want him to, then Rusty is left close to being a dead ass this season. He'll be caught stalking around in the brush with a guide who's holding such a rep he can afford to save himself for his major clients and make the minor executives like Rusty do a little work for him. Rusty has taken a full estimate of Big Luke and has this to decide: man to man, if you put each in the other's job from birth, Rusty could have done everything Luke did except those twenty-five five-shot one-inch offhand clusters, cause that ain't practice, that's magic, and Rusty is modest about magic, but Big Luke in Rusty's shoes would not have gone as far because he might be, bend your head (in secret) too fucking lazy. First thing, smack off, Luke tells Rusty that it's not the best season this year for bear, and when Rusty, all modesty and politeness, allows as how he'd like to make a push against these poor possibilities, Big Luke, who's coming on one hundred out of one hundred relaxed, kind of smiles, crinkly introductory humor humoring, and says, "They're scarce now. When bear get lonesome they can smell far." Well, Big Luke got a presence, not much of a face, just a big sunburned mug of a face like a pie with a lot of scars in it, he looks just like Big Ollie Water Beaver except paler, for Big Ollie is as dark as an old leather jacket, but Big Luke sends out a wave every time he has a thought, you can feel it, and around him you can get messages back, you can feel that one bear out in those woods sending out its message—don't come near, motherfuck—that message transmitted from the bear to Big Luke and relayed to us, you can tune in on the madness in the air, you now know where a pine tree is rotting and festering somewhere out there, and red ants are having a war in its muck, and the bear is listening to those little ant screams and smelling that rotten old pine, and whoong goes his nose into the rot, and he bites and swallows red ants, slap, bap, pepper on his tongue, he picking up the bite of death in each ant and the taste of fruit in the pulp, digging that old rotten tree whose roots tell him where we are, capisce, Luigi? There's a fucking nervous system running through the earth and air of this whole State of Alaska, and the bear is tuned in, and Big Luke, and Ollie and the assistant guide packers, and the ants, and Tex and D.J., and the air, man, the air is the medium and the medium is the message, that Alaska air is real message—it says don't bullshit, buster. And Rusty of course reads this not, cause Big Luke is pouring salt in his ass. Big Luke is *mean*. "Lot of caribou," Big Luke says. "Think about starting the week with caribou." Well, Rusty would as soon start the week with rabbits as caribou deer. D.J. reads this easy—let Rusty presume to come back from the Brooks Mountain Range of Alaska to Big D, Texas, air distance 3,247 miles (check not on this detail, for D.J. has just estimated it—who the mother-butter is going to make such a small-ass measurement of distance but a hotel lobby type tourist?) let Rusty travel all that round trip 6,000 plus miles, spending 6,000 plus dollars on D.J. and himself—not all tax-deductible either, you fuck, and present himself at 4C and P with a deer's head and no bear. Rusty and his status (who are as up tight with each other as two plump yoni—that's Hindu for cunt, son!—doing sixty-nine in the long Hindu night) can now take a double pine box funeral—they'll never got off his ass at Combined Consolidated, no, no, the office staff will wet their little pants waiting for Christmas so they can send him an anonymous set of antlers off some poor ass spavined Texas buck twice the antlers in width of measurement and holding four more points than the one he airfreighted back from Alaska—you know they'll do that at the office if they got to dig up an old ranch hand's bones and glue them together for antlers, Rusty knows a piss cutter when it scratches his scrotum—thank you very much, Mr. Luke Fellinka, but no thanks on that deer.

"Say, Luke," says Rusty, "I sure hope you put the hair on a bear for us cause I'm feeling like the poorest safari victim you've had all year," and Big Luke says, "We, sir, have no safari victims, just happy clients and disappointed clients, and sometimes you can't tell by looking at their face, not by the time they get home."

Bp Berkeles

★
═══════════
═══════════

INTRO BEEP 4

═══════════
═══════════
★

Think of something black-ass and terrible, black as a tumor in your brain, black as the black-ass consciousness of that crippled Harlem genius which D.J. shoves up for gambit as one possible embodiment for his remarkable brain. Shit, shit, and shinola, death in your breath, death in your breath gives a hump to the lung like the silent sound of a pocket turning inside out in the black-ass black-ball closet. Bishop Berkeley, goes the mad comptometer in old D.J.'s head, am I the ideational heat of a real crazy-ass broken-legged Harlem

Spade, and just think myself D.J. white boy genius Texan in Alaska imagining my opposite number in Harlem land, when in fact, Good Lord, when in fact, I, D.J., am trapped in a Harlem head which has gone so crazy that I think I sitting at a banquet in the Dallas ass white-ass manse remembering Alaska am in fact a figment of a Spade gone ape in the mind from outrageous frustrates wasting him and so now living in an imaginary white brain, or is that ether-load man? is not D.J. really white, really walking at sixteen into the vale where the death of breath crosses all eternal wires, and D.J. is merely tapped in for touches of intellectual luxury to some fucked-up little bedridden Spade, or is that the abortive consciousness of a tumor beginning right under the medulla oblongata of his white brain a knot of psychic hatreds congregated in molecule dance to design a new kind of flesh, sarcoma, melanoma, carcinom' and Nome and Barrow, Alaska, Fairbanks—late afternoon?

★
════════════

CHAP FOUR

════════════
★

Well, by the light of the twilight D.J. does a little estimating. There's guides and guides in Alaska, some for scratch-ass hunters, and some for poobahs where the idea is to bring the trophy to the man so that John Foster Dulles types can make the record book without ever getting their cheese wet crossing a brook. By the end of the first night in Fairbanks, while they lolling around getting acquainted in a super deluxe motel bar of a dark chocolate-red velvet interior looks like it was flown up from Seattle (which it was, en route

from Hawaii where they imitating the English Pump
Room in Threadnelly Gate, London W. 1) D.J. and
Tex analyze it out—Big Luke used to be a big hunter,
but those grizzly scratches have weakened his Arnold
Toynbee coefficient—he interested less in challenge
than response—if he caught his share of the three grand
a head without having to lead various grades of assholes and tough but untrained adolescents into the
brush to look for Mr. Wounded Honey Grizzly holding
the head of a magnum in his bear gut and a last dream
of murder in his bear eye, well, Big Luke, despite the
big man death-guts charisma, may have had his day.
Who's to say there is no actors in Alaska?

Listen to the dialogue: "Luke, I'm a stubborn Texas
son of a bitch," says Rusty, lifting his bourbon in the
Fairbanks, Alaska, motel bar (empty near but for three
old couples from Kansas on an airline tour of Anchorage, Fairbanks, Barrow, Nome, and Juneau, with dips
into Kotzebue, Unalakleet, and Homer, and a brother
and sister at University of Alaska entertaining their ma
and pa up to visit from Portland) —this lack of activity
may be given total attributability to the vacation-
directed personal vector imperatives of the American
mind which shuts up action after Labor Day. This is
after Labor Day, early September in Alaska, two years
(to remind you) before the period of D.J.'s consciousness running through his head, hence form is more
narrative, memory being always more narrative than
the tohu-bohu of the present, which is Old Testament

Rimbaud
"Le Gateau"
nove

Hebrew, cock-sucker, for chaos and void, "Yeah, I'm stubborn," sighs Rusty tenderly, sipping his bourbon like his mother had brought him up on mother's milk and moonshine, "I don't want to carry on about where I've hunted, because I could tell you about going for wild boar in Bavaria, and for elephant in Africa—although I never got the elephant, my gun-buddy Ram Fedderstone got it, I just got a kudu, a snake, an African antelope, and a zebra. I always say I paid five thousand—you count them—bucks for a goddam convict suit."

"How about that, Pete?" said M.A. Bill, getting in the big chuckle first.

"Shee-it, Rusty," said M.A. Pete, "that's a beautiful set of head and shoulder zebra stripes in the Bomb Shop" (which is what Rusty calls the Jethroe den, the Bomb Shop).

Rusty turns his head, like a maidenhead being told she's pretty, sort of a "It's not for me to say," and then he turns his keen shit hue executive eyes on Big Luke and says, "I even got in on a tiger hunt with the Maharajah of Pandrasore, but that I don't count because I was present in 'semiofficial function,'" a big wink, man, whatever the fuck semiofficial function is CIA supposed to convey, professor, "and we didn't even carry rifles. There was an array of Hindu peons up ahead each with a kris on a bamboo stick, and they did the sticking. The Maharajah's function, it turns out, is to be some variety of the Great White Hunter.

The majesty of his attendance on the hunt brings tigers up where there were none before. If there's a tiger this side of Tibet the Maharajah's magnetism will draw him. Sure as bird shit on a parasol, damn if we didn't attract three tigers."

"Maybe I get to learn a couple of new things about hunting from you," says Big Luke F.

"Say, Mr. Fellinka, I may look like a variety of Texas bull, but not that big, I swear. No, no, no. I'm not here to instruct, I'm here to imbibe. At the foot of a master. I just want to make a point, teacher. I want to cut the fiercest mustard you ever tasted with a piece of bear steak, I want to behold Bruin right in his pig red eye so I'll never have to be so scared again, not until I got to face The Big Man. Listen, Luke, here's what I suspect is true—it is that you are the Maharajah of this woods and this range of earth, and so I'm expecting you to make the impossible become directly possible and we're going to carry our stretch of hunting to what I would call a successful termination."

"Was a berry blight in August," says Big Luke, "Now the bear are out digging roots in the brush. That's a little thick there. A little too thick to bring a party in. Get a thorn in your eye, gun gets tangled, you can be looking at the ground about the time Friend Bear is putting an arm over your neck."

"Say, now," says Rusty, "this is a guaranteed bear trophy hunt, now isn't it?"

"Well, sir," says Big Luke's Tour Guide Coordi-

nator, Mr. Kenneth Easterly, who has met the group at
the airport, and brought them along Airport Way to the
motel, name now forgotten, Alaska Cavalier maybe, or
Fairbanks Frontier Arms, some such (Fairbanks being
near as flat-ass a city as Dallas has naturally lots of
humper-dick in the names) "well, sir," says Kenneth
E who's the olive oil in this operation, "you have a
guaranteed bear trophy in the specifications of the
safari contract—that's for shit-and-sure," says Easterly,
cause people he's addressing are Texans; if they was
New York Jew ass Banker sportsmen, he'd say "certified." Nods his head, as if he's shaking his hand, "Yessir, there's a rebate of five hundred per head if we
neglect to get you in proper range for a shot at a visible
grizzly, although I want to tell you, we've never had to
rebate it."

"Everybody who's taken your safari has gotten Mr.
Grizzer," asks Rusty, "or had a fair shot?"

"No, sir. Not everybody. Some few do not have that
peculiar good fortune. But they don't want the rebate.
After they see the way Big Luke and Big Ollie take
them around through the Brooks Range—that's
wilderness, Mr. Jethroe—way they cook for 'em, tote
for 'em, skin and pack, they're feeling sufficiently good,
they've had the kind of hunting experience the desire
for which brought them out here in the first place."

Rusty just shakes his head. "I don't believe I follow
you, *boy.*"

"Mr. Jethroe," says Kenny E., "we have the best

63

guide in Alaska, and the finest clientele. We're here to take you around and give you *proper* hunting. We're not in competition with the counters. There are counters out in that wilderness, hunters of medium income (and medium ability to stick the muzzles of their rifles into a muddy piece of ground) who have nonetheless saved their pennies to come here—it's the experience of a lifetime for them, and as you know, sir, the experience of a lifetime excites *greed* in the common man and a terror of being cheated. So they are out to get everything they can. They count every last pelt, they'll twist the tape measuring a Dall's horn to get an extra quarter of an inch on the length of it, they'll use handload cartridges make you gasp—it's a wonder simple steel can stand it—they hunt from four in the morning to midnight before they get back to camp, up at four again, they bring out every last piece of meat they can tote, or they don't even cut themselves a steak, just take the head and leave the flesh, imagine! and they maim, Mr. Jethroe, they maim game all over the damn place and then let them suffer. We ain't like that. We have the finest people in America come to us, we wouldn't even know how to advertise—we just hope too many people don't hear about us or the simple fine standard of clientele we possess might be adulterated. Because we offer hunting which is reasonable, decent in its risk, fair to the game, and not utterly deprived of comfort. We do not consider it decadent to have a book or two in the bunkhouse, and if Big Luke knows how to make a mixed drink, well, whiskey sours sweeten the heart after a long day of hunting, I like to claim."

"That's A-OK," says Rusty, "but the bear is the integral part of this expedition."

"Yessir, it is," says Easterly, "provided the bear is in a reasonable state."

"The bear are bad now," says Big Luke.

"What do you mean bad?"

"Changing their habits," Big Luke says. It comes out. All the good news. It seems there's been too much hunting in the Brooks Range. That's the confession of Kenny Easterly. The Moe Henry and Obungekat Safari Group (which is the exclusive George Humphrey special they are on right now) is no longer so alone in bringing its fine people up into that Arctic Circle, all the counter-type safari groups like Hunting, Ltd., and the Sam Sting Safari are pouring in too. The wild game is changing its psychology.

Big Ollie speaks up—his first speech. He talks like a cannibal in a jungle bunny movie. "Brooks Range no wilderness now. Airplane go over the head, animal no wild no more, now crazy."

"Say, friends," says Rusty, "I didn't come to Alaska to debate the merits and vices of technological infiltration." ✗

Big Luke presents the case: "In August, three grizzly been wounded by other safaris in our hunting range. They get told not to move in but they move in. They,

like you, sir, thought I'm the one to call the tiger so
they hunt near me. They wounded and they neglected
to follow up, and they left us three very mean grizzly,
right in our own hills and lands up there. Now consider. A mean grizzly has only to smell a man and he is
half-crazy. He does not come forward half-nice, half-
mean, to take his look, nor does he go the other way—
he thinks of how to kill. He circles, he stays downwind
from the hunter. He remembers the bullet, that bullet
maybe tore his intestine, that is a terrible pain. A bear
feeling such pain, sir, is in my opinion, struck as if by
lightning and so picking up in certain ways the intelligence of man."

"I see," says Rusty, "you're going to keep us well up
above timber so no bear can sneak near on us. We'll
have to spend our week climbing rocks just to get a shot
at five hundred yards down on some mountain goat
across a canyon."

"I'll give the best hunting for conditions," says
Luke.

"Let's specify," says Rusty.

A sad-ass show. It flickers off, on, off, for ninety
minutes, a muted hot shit hurricane. Finally, Big Luke
hints that Rusty can have his rebate now, his deposit,
his contract and his week, and that is the end of the
first contest, for if there is one thing worse than coming
back with no bear, it is coming back a rejectee and
rebatee from the Moe Henry and Obungekat Safari
Group. If they could satisfy Old General George C.

CHAP FOUR

Marshall in his hunting days, who is Sir Jet-Throne to complain? Now he saves face. He compromises, he agrees Luke will give the word on when they go for grizzer. Say. They all go to bed in rooms with a foam-rubber mattress, pink-tile bathrooms, and Venetian blinds, and in the morning, load gear and all ten men into three Piper Apaches with amphibian floats and take off for the Brooks Range where each plane makes a tasty light water-slap of a landing in a lake, Dolly Ding Bat Lake, where there's an M.H.O.S.G. (for Moe Henry, et cetera) bunkhouse on the shore which is a pine forest so full of boon in the smell it could make you a religious nut, except D.J. does not dig pine resin out of sight–he likes something a hint more funky if he is entering concupiscent relations with the penumbra of the Lord, ho, ho, but this bunkhouse which is a pâté foie of an Alaska bunkhouse is not theirs for long– they unload the planes, then load up on packhorse, and work up a trail all afternoon, a dog ass trail which gets dull and then monotonous dull cause it's pine forest and dwarf birch and not spectacular for being up above the Arctic Circle, Rusty is commenting it's just as dull as all of Canada, and then colors start to dim which gives a hint of some kind of North, cause the rocks have a thin gray, and the bark is gray on the trees and there's a pinched look beginning to appear in the turf, a mossy mean turf like dry bog crusts, the trees get more individual, they have a continuing life story now with the wind. Then timberline. Final timberline, sharp and clean, a little park of grass. They're up high on gray domes looking across to other gray domes, and rising further until even the fold of the canyon is dry of moss, and the packhorses are hawking their breath, and Big Luke finally picks on a shielded-in kind of square saddle between some hunched-up bare knolls, Big Luke calls it a basin, near to a black-ass basin by the time they get there, and put up the tents, Ollie makes the fire, et cetera, roast beef hash with de-hydrated pears, good by God! on a white gasoline cookstove. D.J. and Tex exhausted by the dialectic of the night before fall out into dead-ass air mattress sleep with the smell of the North on a September night, a tricky clean smell, like a fine nerve washed in alcohol and lightly powdered to get the rut of flesh off.

Next morning, on a light windless dawn, Tex and D.J. get out of bed, start to brush their teeth in a rill of a stream coming up out of a mountain spring, that water presenting itself to the teeth like sunlight on snow, and Tex saw, just then, a wolf standing and point-ing a half mile above the timber, just standing there and studying the dawn in a wolf silence like he had come to some conclusion about the problems of life and occupation, near-relatives, in-laws, phratries, asso-ciates, herbs, roots, and grubs. Tex took him down with a shot into the gut and at first he could have been there dead, the animal fell and for an instant the hills clapped together. Down at timberline trees shifted, air moved in the wave which follows a breaking of glass,

and then the wolf was up and running, but with a sick
ass lunge like a broken fly, and then slowed, stood still,
bore off at a bleeding ass walk back to the woods, and
Tex run after him and got him at two hundred yards;
one miss, one hit into the back of the shoulder and the
lungs. The look on Big Luke's face was amiable like
any boy who could hit a wolf at four hundred yards
was not totally undeserving of guided service. Well, he
got down and gave us each a cup of blood to drink and
that was a taste of fish, odd enough, and salt, near to
oyster sauce and then the taste of wild meat like an eye
looking at you in the center of a midnight fire, and
D.J. was on with the blood, he was half-sick having
watched what Tex had done, like his own girl had
been fucked in front of him and better, since he had
had private plans to show Tex what real shooting
might be, and here was Tex, King Front Sight Indian
Hunter, Killer of Wolves. D.J. next thing was on his
hands and knees, looking into that upper Yukon wolf
mouth, those big teeth curved like tusk, and put his
nose up close to that mouth, and thought he was looking up the belly of a whale, D.J. was breathing wolf
breath, the just dead air from the dead interior, but
raucous breath, all the fatigue of the wolf running
broken ass to the woods and the life running the other
way from him, a crazy breath, wild ass odor, something
rotten from the bottom of the barrel like the stink of
that which is unloved, whelp shit smell, wild as wild
garlic, bad, but going all the way right back into the

guts of things, you could smell the anger in that wolf's heart (fucked again! I'll kill them!) burnt electric wire kind of anger like he'd lived to rip one piece of flesh from another piece, and was going to miss it now, going to miss going deep into that feeling of *release* when the flesh pulls loose from the flesh, and there D.J. was sweating, cause he was ready to get down and wrestle with the wolf, and get his teeth to its throat, his teeth had a glinty little ache where they could think to feel the cord of the jugular, it was all that blood he'd drunk, it was a black shit fuel, D.J. was up tight with the essential animal insanity of things.

That, friends, was the beginning of the hunt. Not so bad. Big Ollie came up, asked Tex if he wanted the wolf for a trophy. Tex gave a blow of breath to his front sight. That's all the tension he was going to show. "I don't want no wolf for a trophy," he said. Ollie then studied the animal, nodded, suddenly dipped his finger in the blood, sucked it with a quick-popping sound of his cheek like a cook testing a cake batter, then took out a knife and cut the wolf's head off, one twisting cut of the knife for the vertebra at the neck, one long sawing swinging cut for the rest. Then he gave the head to the boys for a look. There were two eyes open on El Lobo, both yellow coals of light, but one eye was Signor Lupo, the crazy magician in the wolf, and his eye had the pain of the madman who knows there's a better world but he is excluded, and then the other eye, Willie Wolf, like a fox's eye, full of sunlight and peace, a harvest sun on late afternoon field, shit! it was just an animal eye like the glass they use for an eye in a trophy, no expression, hollow peace maybe, and Big Ollie dug a shallow pan of a hole with his knife in the crust bog tundra, whatever that dry shit moss was, and set the wolf's head in it, muzzle pointing to the north, and covered it over. Then he took a broken twig and laid it in a line with the end of the muzzle, but pointing further North, then got down on his hands and knees and touched his nose to the stick and said nothing for a moment.

"Always remember, boys," said Rusty, who had come up at the end to be part of our blood drinkers' breakfast group and coffeeclutch, "you don't get your proper paganism until you pay these dee-luxe prices."

"What he up to, Mr. J.?" said Tex.

"Well, you're looking at him, Indian to Indian, Tex, and don't forget ah got a drop of the fucking redskin elixir too, he's telling that wolf he respects him and not to spread the word, not to get grizzler turned on. I bet Ollie's telling him not to forget that when he was alive, he and Big Grizzler were not rushing to be asshole buddies, so please don't start a union now."

INTRO BEEP 5

That's it about a High-Grade A.H.—they can surprise you by times. D.J. is thus proud of his dad for filling Tex in that he could almost revise his opinion of Rusty if it wasn't for his Big Daddy's shit-licking propensity to have a chameleon pussy sphincter changeling of a voice—get Rusty out in the woods and he's Texas ass, man, common as dirt, hard as nails, he could crunch a clamshell with his asshole, rolls his prejudices around in his throat like a fat cricket in honey—but insert him behind a dinner table with candles, tablecloth, nubian

"memors is the seed of narrative"
"the inside of the brain is always the present"

black-ass Washington, D.C. type Pullman Porter but-
lers (Hallelujah actually has one working steady which
leaves most of the North Dallas hostesses stricken into
electrified shit, for, man, they got a scale for how rash
and rough and poor white redneck raw yore lady's
ass still is, and Hallelujah obviously got skin on her
butt as sweet as the average plump dear woman has
on her full sail of tits.) Yeah! Butter wouldn't melt in
Hallelujah's butt, and you could think Rusty was but-
tering his bread in the same ingredient at a dinner table
(where this reminiscence of hunting began sometime
ago to run in narrative form) because, Repeat, all you
deficient heads out there and nascent electronic grop-
ers, memory is the seed of narrative, yeah, and D.J.
grassed out at a formal dinner in his momma daddy's
Dallas house with Tex in white smoking jacket across
the table has brought back gobs of Alaska hunt memory
two years before including the critical contrast in
Rusty's voice between down home talk (biggest Texas
ass accent in the corporation) and Cosmo high-fashion
dinner talk, gentry ass style, no ideas, but a thousand
fine names. Tonight they're entertaining the ex American Ambassador from Bringthatpore, shit! old lover
of Halleloo's and various North Dallas matrons (street
names on request) who got a Roman candle up their
ass on what might come up in Death-row Jethroe's
southern manse this eve. This is two years later, right
now, but the inside of the brain is always the present
even if it is memory two years old, and wolf blood

74

drunk that morning like wine is the up and Adam of D.J.'s racing or expiring consciousness up now right in the Brooks Mountain Range, and what has happened after the wolf is that one of the medium assholes, Pete, in fact, has just wounded a caribou, right where they're all standing looking at Signor Lupo's old magician wolf grave, and he has done it with a horror head of a gun and cartridge, wait and hear, and everybody's ass is now triple slung, cause they got to get up from the wolf without breakfast and track that wounded caribou. Poor Medium Asshole Pete.

CHAP FIVE

Well, now here, let's give a rundown on the guns for those good Americans who care. And those who don't, shit, they still get the chance to encounter a lot of meaningless names and numbers which they can then duly repeat at cocktail parties for new name grabbers.

Rusty, well now he's got, well you be sure Rusty is holding, in fact D.J. is now canny to save him for later. So here's Luke and Ollie. Luke got a Model 70 Winchester .375 Magnum restocked (with maple Japa-

nese Shigui finish) and remodeled by Griffin & Howe
with a Unertl 2½× scope, and that little rifle and
cartridge could knock down anything but an elephant,
and if the elephant had just gotten fucked, it would
knock him down too. Luke don't need that gun, he
could hit and take and flatten anything he wanted in
Alaska with his second gun, old Swedish Husqvarna
.30-06, restocked and remodeled, also Unertl 2½×
scope (Luke was agent for Unertl for a while) which
handles a 180-grain bullet on a very flat trajectory, a real
300–400 yard bap of an ice picker, extra high up over 3
thou in velocity delivered at the muzzle. Whereas Ollie
has the same gun D.J. has, a factory-bought Remington
721, and both he and D.J. have worked the stock
themselves. Ollie has all kinds of ivory totems and
taboos inset in his grip and comb, including a profile
of wolf head (hot shit and coincidence, Claudia!) and
he got a nice Lyman Alaska 2½× scope. D.J. on his side
has just done a little stupid ass inconclusive whittling
into his Rem 721 stock—in truth it's a mess—forget it!
Scope? He got a nice Stith Bear Cub 2½× scope with
Stith mounts.

Tex has a factory-bought Winchester .270 Model 70
with a Weaver K-3 Tilden mount, neat as that. If he
was a fink, D.J. would whisper that the first 400
yard shot which hit the wolf, considering it was done
with a good .270 like the Winchester 70, was nothing
truly spectacular, for Tex had set his Weaver K-3 for
250 yards the day before when they crossed timberline.

So, at 400 yards, even with a big 180-grain bullet (and the corresponding big-ass load of powder) he knew he wouldn't drop twenty inches below the cross hair, never, at four hundred yards, so it wasn't that hard to put the dot a bit above wolf's back and hit in eight inches or ten inches below his spine. Anyway the whole fucking kill was unaesthetic, cause a 180-grain bullet which lets a wolf walk away after hitting him must hit no closer than a red-hot poker along his ass. Fact, that's what on examination the first shot proved itself to be, for the weight and hard nose of the bullet (bought to penetrate a grizzly hide) went right through the wolf's two legs, breaking only one. Well this fine critique ain't just piss grapes from D.J., because proof is that he is now repeating Tex Hyde's very own critique of his own shot. "If I hadn't been fever ass," says Tex, "I'd have taken the time and got the 100-grain soft nose magazine into Winnie, and I could have torn a hunk of old Wolf right out of his heart so he didn't have to suffer and we didn't have to chase. I can hit *anything* with the hundred grain. That was a fink and fuckup kill, D.J."

Which brings up Rusty, who travels like a big-ass hunter. That Apache looked like it was vomiting big equipment out of its guts, yeah, he got for instance a .404 Jeffrey on a Mauser Magnum action with a Circassian walnut stock, one love of a custom job by Biesen with Zeiss Zielklein 2½× on Griffin & Howe side mount for Gun #1. Gun #2 is Model 70 Win-

chester rechambered to .300 Weatherly Magnum, Stith
Bear Cub scope, bird's-eye maple stock, et cetera,
et cetera. Gun #3 is Winslow Regimental Grade 7
mm. Remington Magnum with FN Supreme 400
action and Premium Grade Douglas barrel, ivory and
ebony inlays in the stock, basket weave carving on both
sides of the forearm and pistol grip, Redfield Jr.
mounts, Redfield 2×-7× variable scope.

Gun #4 is Ruger . . .

Gun #5 . . .

Forget it. This account has now come right down to
the gnat in the navel of the whole week of hunting
which is Sweet Medium Sweet Asshole Pete who don't
know about hunting enough to go out and shoot at
Texas cactus (which, if you know how to plug it
proper, dies with a scream of Pulque blood gushering
up and out and an absolutely foul breakwind of Peyote
gas) no, Pete has grown up with a nice Savage 99 lever
action .250 deer gun, and he runs and freezes his own
scared hot shit in a suburban rental frozen food locker
when he gets the invitation to Alaska from Rusty, for
that means a two- to five-year expediting of his danger-
ously dull slick as owl shit ascent of the corporation
ladder provided he can make it on this Yukon expedition. So he runs out and he borrows a Savage 110 bolt
action with Weaver K-4 scope from his deadly daddy
(who years ago never thought enough of Pete's shooting to give him the 110, but laid, instead, the 99 lever
action on him for Christmas). Well, that takes one

nightmare out of Pete's head which is cocking that 99
fuck-your-finger lever while a grizzly, perfectly capable
of eating whatever the Savage 99 .250 will throw,
ambles and slides and tears across the brush at him.
And it warms his heart cockles, cause it's the first
treasured thing his daddy ever loaned him. (His daddy's
beginning to breathe thin.) Well, Pete now starts hear-
ing about the bolt action 110. It will stop any game,
yeah, if the shot is *well placed*. Strangle that little news.
Pete ain't looking to make a career of placing his
supershots in superb array anywhere but in the office
jungle. Don't tell him about 180-grain Core-Lokt or
Silver Tipt, he wants a grenade and bullet all in one
sweet cartridge package—he wants a bomb which will
drop a grizzly if it hits him in the toe. So he what?
Better believe! Comedy is the study of the unsound
actions of the cowardly under stress, just as tragedy is
equal study time of the brave under heroic but enig-
matic, reverberating, resonant conditions of loss—yes,
professor, you may keep the change, for D.J. is, mean
to say, *has* got more than a finger into the cunt of
genius, Madame Muse. He has now to tell you that
poor Very Low-Grade Medium Asshole Pete is so
squash-breathed at the ups and downs of careerman-
ship and sudden death which now confront him that he
buys—get in line to look at it—from a white-haired
riverboat string-tie type of an ex oil well promoter,
some friend of his wife's shiftless uncle's boss, a third-
string Dallas Mafia type (don't even look how that gun

got around to there or the Ford Foundation will be up
and along for gropes) this gun being a used, indeed
banged-up, African rhinoceros-hippo-elephant-soften-
the-bullet-for-the-lion double-barreled .600–.577 custom, only-one-of-its-kind-ever-built Jeffrey Nitro Express carrying a 900-grain bullet for Shot #1, a 750-
grain for Shot #2, and a recoil guaranteed to knock a
grand piano on its ass. Forget about the French walnut
and the Jeffrey action, the Hensoldt Zielklein 2¾X
scope interchangeable with the Redfield 2X-7X blunt
picket post with cross wire variable scope on the
Pachmayr Lo-Swing mount or the addition of the
Lyman aperture in the 17A front sight on the .577
barrel to be used when the rhinoceros is so close,
friends, that the use of a telescopic sight is not indi-
cated (which means, Herbert, that you better put the
muzzle in your mouth and blast that rhino horn right
back out of your ass). Yeah! This was the gun F. Lap-
Ass Medium Asshole Pete brought to Alaska for
grizzly. When he saw it, Rusty had a pure shit fit. If it
hadn't been a Jeffrey he'd have laughed his nuts off.
But, fix on this, Rusty thought he had the only big
bore Jeffrey in the State of Texas, and here was his
flunky with a bigger, and *double!* . . .

"How'd you get this mother-fuck?" he asked Pete. "I
haven't heard of a double Jeff Nite Express since they
used it to kill a Swiss dragon who was terrorizing some
Tyrolean village in 1921."

"Somebody sold it to me," Pete confesses.

"Well, I hope you didn't pay too much, because the fellow must have stolen it."

In fact, Pete has bought it for $1,000 heart-hurting bucks. A swindle and a crime. The two barrels are thus crooked they could shoot each other. Pore Pete, Be Your Boss Pete, has had already to lay out near to $4,200 bucks for this Brooks Range safari-and-*gun* and has thus had to sell his #2 car, a somewhat used Jag XKE for three big ones plus another thou by converting some Dreyfus Fund into straight cash. He wouldn't dare sell his Pure Pores debentures, no, nor go further into installment debt.

Well, Rusty is in a marching state of perturbation. The very presence of that gun seems enough to shatter the tissue or texture of the spell which hangs over every happy hunter. Up in the basin, by the fire, night before the morning Tex killed the wolf, Big Luke has taken one look at Pete's possession and Rusty knows what he is thinking: this is one extrafine gaggle of goose fat and asshole to contend with for a week. So Rusty attacks. He knows enough to get attention off that Nitro Express! He inquires after Big Ollie's second gun, knowing pure well there is only the Remington 721, Big Ollie is a man for an all-purpose rifle, and when Big Luke says, "Ollie take care of everything with one gun," Rusty says, "Yeah, well why're you carrying a .375?"

"Ollie can back you up just as well with that .30-06."

"You know a .30-06 isn't going to do the job of a .375 Magnum. It wasn't *designed to*," says Rusty, getting a good old Texas range whine like the ricochet of a bullet off a stupid-ass Texas desert rock. He is obviously thinking of Mr. Grizzer. What Big Luke is thinking is not so far from conjecture. He is either (a) carrying a .375 to make his clients happy, since he shoots good enough to stop anything with a .30-06, a #.270, even a .245 if he got to, or (b) he has lost more nerve than Ollie, so he has more power in his fire stick. Either way, he got to protect Ollie and his one gun, he ain't getting in a situation where he might have to tell #2 man what sort of gun said #2 is supposed to sling in order to keep Sir Jet-Throne happy.

Rusty knows all this too, but he hasn't put in the years being a first-line Ranger Commando in 4C and P for zero return, he knows how to keep an expert on the defensive (and remind him of a nightmare or two) by poking in just hard enough to the mysteries between the facts. "Listen," says Rusty, "nobody knows finally what's going to kill big game. Some seem to go over if you put a pin in their butt, others you take right through the heart—they keep running. Running right at you if need be."

"Shoot for the shoulder, not the heart," says Big Luke in a voice like a piece of old oiled gunstock, a voice with a patina—he has said this two thousand times over the years.

"Right," says Rusty, "the shoulder. Break the shoulder bone, and they can't run. Sure. That's where I want my power. Right there. Right then. Maybe a professional hunter takes pride in dropping an animal by picking him off in a vital spot—but I like the feeling that if I miss a vital area I still can count on the big impact knocking them down, killing them by the total impact, shock! it's like aerial bombardment in the last Big War," he said, turning to Tex, D.J., and the Medium Assholes, and dropping his voice as if he were now imparting the flavor of the secret jellies and jams used in black mass of real military lore, "why, face up, gentlemen, the British were right, hear, hear, they were right for once, you don't pinpoint vital areas in a city, you blot it all out, you bury it deep in fire, shit, and fury. Then when the war's over they're glad to see you come in. It's just like if you get in a fight with a fellow, you're well advised to destroy him half to death. If y'get him down, use your shoe on his face, employ your imagination, give him a working-over, hard to believe, but often enough that man is your friend afterward, you've made him sane—maybe he thought before he had the fight with you he could lick whatever was in sight so he was half-crazy, now he knows that is not exactly so. Whereas if you give him a nice clean whipping, you've stimulated him to give you a nice clean whipping back. Of course, the analogy is not perfect, Luke, but I am forced to wonder about the fine difference in ethics between using Ollie's .30-06, and my Special .404, or your .375. Yes, it may be our

WHY ARE WE IN VIETNAM?

animals will die a degree more from shock and a hint
less from vital execution. But of what final ethical
consequence is that, where is the fine difference?"

"Your meat tastes better when you're executed,"
said Tex.

Big Luke gave a laugh, Rusty gave a look at the
undertaker's son. "Let me just tell you," he said into
the fire, "I hope I don't have to stand on tiptoe too
long waiting for you, Tex, to squeeze a needle out of
your .270."

"You won't," said Tex.

Well, M.A. Pete heard all of this and more, he heard
from his tentmate M.A. Bill a little later that night, for
Bill was a ballistics nut and had spent one full vacation
in the ballistics department of the FBI in the Department of Justice building in D.C. (having used the
influence of his boss Death-row Jelly-Go Jet-Throne
and the friendship of some of the local FBI to be
accepted as a guest-visitor and temporary student on
the comparative rank basis of police captain so that
M.A. Bill got his studying in with visiting foreigners
like the head of the Ghana Police Department, and the
Mozambique Police Department, and native fuzz from
Spokane, Walla Walla, Greensboro—they were all taking the full invitation and orientation course in up-
dated police detection methods, but M.A. Bill was no
investigator manqué, rather he was a ballistics nut, and
that's where he stayed for two hot blazing summer
weeks in the air-conditioned laboratories of the bal-

86

listics boys). He'd always gone in for handloading his cartridges, but when he got back, he was abruptly become the cartridge expert in his rifle club cause he could advise you on the FBI selection and use of bullets, primer, case, shot, and powder, he was up on the latest Department of Justice methods of determining chamber pressure, mean effective pressure, hunting loads, reasonable uses for black powder, new powders, flash holes, bullet castings, bullet swaging, etc., he had a spread of loading tools, dies, accessories, components, lathes, and was therefore all equipped to wildcat his own. Some of them were pretty hot. M.A. Bill had been known to come into the office with gunpowder injected in his pores, but a breech had never blown up in his face. Of course, no dentist has love for a doctor, and no wildcatter has a good word for a factory cartridge. M.A. Pete had been ready after Rusty's contumely to bury his Jeffrey Nitro Express and make the trip with the Savage 110 .30-06, but M.A. Bill squared him off on that. He let him in on the secret—factory ammunition was the unspoken scandal of American life, and .30-06, well in M.A. Bill's opinion, they were the worst offenders. The f.p.s. (foot per second, knothead!) variations had been known to go up to 5 percent, and one box in not that very many you'd be surprised had such variations and fluctuations in their max. vel., as tested on the chronograph that trajectories could even be affected. Which meant? Pete wanted to know. Errors in shooting, said M.A. Bill.

WHY ARE WE IN VIETNAM?

D.J. is here to tell you that M.A. Pete wished to hear no more, which was error indeed, cause a little cross-examination would have revealed that M.A. Bill was talking about a difference which was not an inch at one hundred yards, not by half. You see, fellow Americans, statistics perverts, and number addicts, the greatest effect of variation in powder loadings speaks up after you go by the sign which says, "You are a rifle bullet passing the three-hundred-yard mark and are bound soon to dip. Keep your nose up!" In fact, M.A. Bill like most ballistics nuts was as nearsighted as an old hound with silver rim lenses so his critique is academic for himself. He's not interested in where the bullet goes, he just wants to stuff it full of the right sort of smokeless. Love, love, the Good Lord may have had no idea how far he cast his seed.

"But your gun is a .30-06," says M.A. Pete.

"Yes, but I've had it rechambered and with a custom barrel. I make my own shell for it. A .311. I wouldn't ever use a .30-06."

"Oh," said Pete, "that .311 must really do the job."

"You can go to sleep on that," said M.A. Bill.

M.A. Pete did not sleep too well. He had visions of a grizzly bearing down on him with a wild cry like a Nigger washerwoman gone ape with a butcher knife, and he had seen himself forced to face such music with the slim pencil of a .30-06. He had had dreams of bringing it off with a .30-06 but that buried scandal of American sporting rifle cartridge ammo f.p.s. discrep-

ancies recounted to him by M.A. Bill had the front
sight of his Savage 110 wavering like a fly wing in his
mind's eye. If the aim of the bullet could not be
trusted, then of what purport the gun? So, fuck if he
didn't have his hand on the double Jeffrey all night
long and kiss your own ass deep in the heart of Texas if
the elephant gun wasn't the tool that M.A. Pete
brought with him when he went running down into
the valley and the green park of lawn below the black-
ass gray basin, down in the sweet green grass right after
Tex shot his wolf, that grass green as an English lawn,
just where the trees ended and the mountain went up
in a gray dome. And standing around, looking at the
dead wolf, he looked up, and he, the medium asshole,
was the first to see a caribou two hundred yards away
through the thin trees, and in the accurate fevered
inaccuracy of being awake a night without sleep, he
took a sight and the cross hairs on the scope ran a figure
eight around the horns, which then plummeted down
around the hooves, flew up past the tail into the air,
about, and back over the caribou's flanks to a view, all
abrupt, honest, naked, and hairy of the buck's testicles
magnified 4×, which to M.A. Pete's unprotected eye
was equal in force and simple animal revelation to the
first sight provided an innocent maiden of a working-
man's balls, and then past caribou's deer nuts in a blur
as if M.A. Pete was in a movie traveling the curves so it
was all a blur, and around came the sights again to the
back of the hocks and up and RUMBA! went the Jeffrey

and the .600 Nitro Express shot on its way and M.A. Pete took a blow to the shoulder on recoil which canted his vertebrae 3 degrees 21 minutes right then and there, and Wow! came a sound next to him, for the caribou leaped in the air, did a crazy dance, and was off in the woods.

★

INTRO BEEP 6

★

Well, D.J.'s consciousness must be expiring in the brackish backwaters of a sluggish narrative, for we have been hung up in numbers, details, and all sorts of overspecific technical data as if it were scum, slime, pollen slick, floating twigs, and wet rotting leaves all meandering down a dead-ass stream, but, man, you leave those paved streets and get your ass flown abruptly from the high technological nexus and overdeveloped civilization of a megacity like the Dallas–Fort Worth complex into a riptide impact and collision area margi-

nated halfway between civilization and a nature cul-
ture-primitive constellation (like Alaska, man) and
then intensify such culture shock by inserting the sub-
jects (1 H.A., 2 M.A., and 2 TA½T) —which latter
stands for Tex and D.J. (2 Tough Adolescents ½
Tested) —well, you might just as well sing along with
the Rotten Moss and the Red Hots, Yeah, I Got an
Itching in My Palm Which Some Call Love, because
that's shock, Mr. Buzz-buzz, up from Dallas into the
Brooks Range, and boys like Rusty and the M.A.s all
being men, there's just nothing to do with Mr. Anxiety
but carry him around in place of Herr Dread, and hang
out those numbers, Harvey, don't forsake those names,
Nelson, remember that being up from Dallas so abrupt
makes a man feel small and modest like he's full of shit,
so give a little Christian bomb, spelled b-a-l-m, and
forgive and forget that slow smelly backed-up hardly
moving narrative stream of facts, figures and general
meaningless horseshit which D.J. has been feeding, and
fix your eye on the white stumpy tail and sweet white
ass of the buck caribou up and bounding away and
now the problem is to track him.

★

_____

CHAP SIX

_____

★

D.J., your presumptive philosopher, has not made the grand connection yet between the balls and the ears although he would claim they are related—more of this later, maybe—but the eyes are of course attached to the asshole as begining is to end: the end is putting something out—the beginning is to see what you are going to have to shit out, and that right here in Brooks Range is easy to know because it will be the recollection of the blood on the cotton white ass of that caribou just hit by M.A. Pete. A liver-vitiating sight, Carter, for the liver goes flat, D.J. would assure you, whenever some scent meets its deodorant, or an herb is fed with aspirin. Pretty literary for adolescent out hunting with Paw? Go fuck, D.J.'s got his purchase on the big thing—genius—and he know this: you deaden a mystery and your liver goes to shit. This chase for a torn-ass caribou revolves around a simple mystery, to wit the ass of the caribou is white, its stumpy tail is white, soft as a white ruffle at Milady Hightits throat, so D.J. ask you why? Why is the rear view of a thousand head of caribou passing on the tundra like a thousand pops of cotton on the boll? That's a dead-ass question—the ass of your mind go dead trying to answer, yeah, and here was just one caribou, off on a split through the woods. But we all had one look, one crack of a look at something red and hanging bad and loose like a wattle from the white fur. Then we were all walking and jogging down an open aisle of moss-green grass to the spot in the timber two hundred fifty yards below where the deer had plunged in.

Blood for his trail, drops the size of every kind of coin, silver dollars up to florins, even—one the size of a small plate—brown blood already corrupted by a hive of near invisible devourers, insect shitters, chiggers and flies, one big Alaska bumblebee still alive on this cold early September morning, and the sun shining right in the blood with a thousand lights, or so it would look if you had your nose right there on the bloodied leaves close enough to that wet to think you were looking at

94

neon signs, the woods were full of awe, nothing other, the trees standing numb, cowardly spectators, man, watching one of their own take a wasting.

Then the trail of the blood took a bend, beat through dwarf alder, and some nasty kind of brush with too much in the way of catbriers. That took quite a few minutes, then a pine grove, then another aisle between trees, parallel to the one we had come down, but now the caribou trail was rising up to timberline again, and in the distance, up along a thousand yards, was what looked to be the caribou, yes, it was, and through the field glasses Big Luke, watching, shook his head. "You hit him an outside rump shot, Pete."

"Then he'll be all right?"

"No, impact seems to have broke his leg or maybe shocked his spine. He's using only one hind leg. Walking not much faster than us. That's bad. We can't leave him."

"Say," said Pete, trying to shift the rump of the subject, "why'd that buck leave timber?"

"Didn't want to die in those woods. Sometimes you get a buck will cross three open ridgelines to get into the particular woods where he wants to hide or give it up."

"Then he ain't too bad if he can move that much."

"He," said Big Luke, "is bad enough that we got to get him."

It was going to take all day. We were going to spend our first day walking and jogging to chase a wounded

caribou, when there were ten thousand head of them
in the Brooks Range. All honors due to M.A. Pete's
Jeffrey Nitro Express. Well, Luke got the helicopter
up. It had been down in Fairbanks for repair the day
before, he had not mentioned how near it was to reach,
oh no, he did not want to have Rusty on his ear all
those hours of the packtrain up the mountain from
Dolly Ding Bat Lake, but now he took us up the aisle
through the trees till we were above timber again and
led us along a shallow canyon and over a saddle into
our basin, and there while breakfast was made by one
of the flunky packer guide cooks, Ed Smith, an Indian,
Big Luke got a big-ass walkie-talkie 3200 RC-1A
16 mile range, and rang down to camp at the lake
telling them to come on in, and when they did with a
smack of static, he told them to bring the helicopter
on up.

That's how they got Kid Caribou. Helicopter pilot
was there in five minutes with Buster Bubbletop, a real
wasp of a Bell helicopter, and Big Luke got in with
M.A. Pete and M.A. Pete's cannon, and they zipped up
and over the ridge, and Rusty, and Tex, and D.J. went
to the top of a knoll and followed them with Rusty's
Hurdle & Reuss 7 × 35 and Tex and D.J.'s own Jap
Titan 8 × 35 and Binolux 7 × 35. And, man, this is
what they see—half dead ass caribou climbing up those
rocks, nice head of antlers (look to be fourteen points
through the glass) and a bleeding jagged gored red ass,
flap of flesh now wide open, and the caribou makes

those rocks with lunge and grunt and like then a
whimper you could hear almost through the binocs
when the sound of the helicopter began to beat on
caribou ear with rings of ether just as when you going
out on the operating table. Man, that caribou looks as
dogged and frantic as a prospector climbing a mountain to get a hill of gold, and then the helicopter is on
top of him and hovering and holding him frozen, and
it lands not fifty feet away, and the caribou turns his ass
and starts to climb up a cliff with a set of deliberate
steps like (1) fuck you, (2) go kill, (3) shit on you, each
step a pure phrase of the blues—take me away, Mr.
Dixieland—and there is M.A. Pete stepping out gin-
gerly from the copter, like, man, he's *close* to the
caribou, and got his cannon with him, and just as Old
Buck Broken Ass gets to the top of his little cliff,
hopping slow on three legs, M.A. Pete sends a Nitro
Express up into his gut from the rear, right into the
red mask of the old wound and that animal does a
Geländesprung right into the air as if his spine is
illumined in incandescence, and somersaults in the air,
and falls twenty feet from the cliff, smashing one set of
antlers off his head (to be wired on later, nothing
other) and the .600 900-grain blasted through his intes-
tines, stomach, pancreas, gallbladder, liver and lungs,
and left a hole to put your arm in, all your arm, up to
the shoulder if you are not squeamish, entrail
swimmer, and then bullet breaking, some of the fragments ripped into the brain and out the head, leaving

97

it scarred to the point where M.A. Pete could claim
(and believe) two years later that the scars on the
mouth and face of his deer trophy were the fighting
marks of a big buck caribou fighter; other fragments
sawed through the ribs of the lungs, and deteriorated
like buckshot in the forequarter. Big Luke brought
that animal back to feed us. Its guts, belly and lungs
were one old jelly flung together by the bullets, one
blood pudding of a cocktail vibrated into total promis-
cuity by the twenty-foot fall down the rocks. Yes,
prince, yes, Big Luke got the head off, and rescued the
loose antler, and gutted the entrails, dressed the meat
to clean fragments, left the hide which was a mess—
clear surprise, yes!—but we had the meat for lunch,
and it wasn't exactly gamy, it tasted loud and clear of
nothing but fresh venison steeped in bile, shit, and the
half-digested contents of a caribou's stomach—it was so
bad you were living on the other side of existence,
down in poverty and stink wallow with your nose
beneath the fever—that was Luke's message to us.

The helicopter was new to him, you read, and for
some parties in the last year or so he'd begun to use it,
for some not, but he was an American, what the fuck,
he had spent his life living up tight with wilderness
and that had eaten at him, wilderness was tasty but
boredom was his corruption, he had wanted a jolt, so
sees it D.J., Big Luke now got his kicks with the
helicopter. He was forever enough of a pro not to use it
with real hunters, no, man, but he had us, gaggle of

98

goose fat and asshole, killers of bile-soaked venison, so
the rest of the hunt, all next seven days he gave what
was secretly wanted, which was helicopter heaven, and
it was curious shit, all rules and regulations, for of
course we did not hunt from the air, no freakmen from
TV land us, but rather noble Dallasassians, so we
broke open a war between us and the animals, and the
hunt hills of the Moe Henry and Obungekat Safari
patch rang with ball's ass shooting, the real breeze,
hopping to the top of a mountain on copter wings to
shoot down on goats, nothing so great as the Alaska
mountain goat, yeah, you get up at three A.M. in tent
camp up high above timber, and you climb, man, on
foot above timber, for three hours till dawn, and then
climb higher still crabbing up sixty-degree rock slopes,
and walking with all heart shit up in your throat along
a ledge twelve inches or less, yeah, ooh, making it up,
and higher still, *quietly,* and then if you good, you're
up there, up above Master Mountain Goat, and when
you start to shoot on him, he does a step dance like an
old Negro heel-and-toe tap man falling down stairs or
flying up them, and the first animal D.J. got in Alaska
was a mountain goat at two hundred and fifty yards,
and with one shot, animal stood on its nose for one
long beast of a second, and then did a running dying
dance for fifty yards down the rocks like a fakir sprint-
ing through flaming coals, and when he died, *Wham!*
the pain of his exploding heart shot like an arrow into
D.J.'s heart, and the animals had gotten him, they were

talking all around him now, communicating the unspoken unseen unmeasurable electromagnetism and
wave of all the psychic circuits of all the wild of Alaska,
and he was only part of them, and part he was of
gasoline of Texas, the asshole sulfur smell of money-oil
clinging to the helicopter, cause he had not gotten that
goat by getting up in the three A.M. of morning and
climbing the mountain, no cream not your dear private lace, dear Celia, D.J. had gotten up at seven back
in the bunkhouse at Dolly Ding Bat Lake, for once Big
Luke had decided this was Helicopter Week for Goose
Fat Gaggle, he bundled all souls and A-holes back to
the bunkhouse since good old Hail the Cop Turd
could take you a day's walk in ten minutes, and he
would drop us on spots, top of a mountain, edge of a
bull moose pond, across a canyon from Dall ram, near
a feeding ground for the grizzer, that copter was divid-
ing us up, carrying us here, there, every which spot,
shooting in parties of two and four, guide and guest, or
two guides, two guests, and it was a haul of big-ass
game getting, for among the five of us safari payers we
had a limit of twenty-five assorted grizzly, moose, ram,
goat and caribou, and there was animal steaks being
cut and packed all over the place, and trundled out by
copter back to Dolly Ding Bat and up again in Super
Cub to Fairbanks and freezers, all that hot supersensi-
tive game meat now locked in brown paper and stone
ice, paralyzed stiff in a freezer, about to suffer for sins it
could not locate, yes, that was how D.J. got his moun-

tain goat, he was flown at seven in the morning up to
the top of a spiky ridge not too unlike the moon, set
down in a bowl with Tex, Ollie, and Kenny Easterly,
and waited, and in two hours had his shot, had his
action, climbing down a ravine, and up the other side,
a walk of four hundred yards, had his work helping Big
Ollie skin, butcher, gut and package Mr. Goat (being
shown by Ollie how to keep the fur away from the
meat so the taste would not be tainted—touch of goat
skin on raw goat meat smelling as stale and raunchy as
overworked whore) and then Big Ollie having radioed
the copter, in came the Hail the Cop and let down a
line all hovering and they slung the meat packages, and
the horns and head onto the lift line, which pulled it
up and then pulled them up—that was the kick of the
morning, foot in the stirrup, lifting one hundred feet
to the Cop Turd which vibrated above like one giant
overgrown Hog! its carburetor farting, its motor giving
out that family sputter of gasoline being piston-cooked
at medium speed, but D.J. never looked at the head of
the goat except once, for the goat had a clown's expression in his little-ass red dying eyes, the fires of the heart
working to keep custard on the clown's face, it wasn't
until that night when he was in the bunkhouse back at
Dolly Ding Bat that D.J. relaxed enough to remember
that goat picking his way up and down rocks like a slow
motion of a skier through slalom, his legs and ass swinging opposite ways, carefree, like take one leg away, I'll
do it on the other, and it hit D.J. with a second blow on

WHY ARE WE IN VIETNAM?

his heart from the exploding heart of the goat and he sat up in bed, in the bunk, listening to the snores, stole out to the night, got one breath of the sense of that *force* up in the North, of land North North above him and dived back to the bed, his sixteen-year-old heart racing through the first spooks of an encounter with Herr Dread.

What more you want to hear? They got them all, crazy caribou trophy heads, eighteen-point buck for M.A. Bill, M.A. Bill! his handload .311 cartridge did the job, and tore off the ass—D.J. will not dwell on why an asshole is bound to hit the ass, for that is homeopathic magic, man—we got it all, that helicopter made us like a bee pulling honey from flower after flower, moose and goose if there'd been goose, and Dall ram, horns and horns of Dall ram, all five of us in three teams got to blast our own set of horn before one day was done on a herd up in a sink near a pinnacle, and Big Luke's Cop Turd pilot was pushing the rules and regs of Hail Cop hunting, for after he lower us out on the line which had even Rusty close to involuntary defecation (and was the most heroic thing corporation execs have done in many a year), why, we got left set up two hundred yards from old herd of Dall ram, Mr. and Mrs. Beautiful Ibex horn (that's Jew horn, I Beck'n Son, hih, hih) ain't got the curl and spiral of the universe curving out of their brain for nothing, they took up and off, and Mr. Cop Turd went swinging after them like a darning needle after ladybugs and

102

CHAP SIX

headed the Dall ram off till they started to run back
toward us, at which point he cut them off again (by
crossing in front of them only thirty feet above—kick
hump in this hunting is: be Cop pilot) since unwritten
Copt. rules and regs forbid chasing of game into gun,
at which point Dall ram leader was like to be very
confused and hit out this way and that way, and the
Cop just went circling around until the sheep were
fixed, shit they were hypnotized, it was pretty to watch,
cause Hail Cop was like a bullfighter twisting a bull
through the limits of his neck until he just got to stand
and wait and let his neck recover, and the copter
having the herd of Dall ram finally fixed on a cleft in a
ridge across a bare modest draw from us, us hiding in
the rocks on the lip of the sink, he pulled up and out,
each circle a little bigger than the one before, and now
a little higher until the animals shivering from the
release of anxiety, in fact all strung out from the sound
of air boiling, breaking, roaring and tearing and the
whine—what cry of what beast?—were able to do no
more than walk around, hocks trembling, muzzles
nuzzling assholes—like get back to that flesh, man!
they must have felt they were being born out again.

I got the first shot. Kneeling behind a rock with a
moss hummock not larger than the hand for a rest, it
all felt good, I had gotten so hypnotized myself, there
was no fever looking through the scope, the eye picked
on one ram standing on one rock all four legs together
and head silhouetted out against a sawtooth ridge

103

maybe five miles behind him, and in the scope I had
one look at the prettiest face D.J. has ever seen,
almond oval and butter love for eyes, a little black
sweet pursed mouth, all quivering now, two nostrils
cunning as an old Negro witch smelling gypsy money
on a mark, whoo-ee—I got the dot above my reticule in
the center of the curl of the horn—those horns went
three hundred and sixty degrees around the ear, like
holding the mountain in the palm of your hand, they
were receptors to hear the curve of the wind in the
private cave of the mountains about, they were a coil of
horn around the nerve which tunes the herb, and
D. Ramses was all horned in on me, hair to the left, hair
to the right went his head, we could just as well have
been pulling opposite ends. I could not help it, want-
ing to keep that head intact for a trophy, the scope still
would not leave the horn, the dot stayed on the ram
brain, one inch above the eye, and feeling like the
instant before the jump first time off a garage roof, D.J.
pulls his trigger finger, perfect pull, perfect shot, as if
all spiral of horn was funnel to pull all of the aim in
and the shot went in one inch above the eye and the
animal went down like a wall had fallen, best shot D.J.
ever made, and Rusty rushed in his shot, cause his
sheep took off at D.J.'s shot, Rusty only wounded his
beast, got a second blast away too high in the shoulder,
off with a third in the hoof—believe it if you want—
the hoof later as splattered from the .404 as a wad of tar
beaten with a hammer, and finally got him in the

shoulder near the heart, the animal not moving hardly now, was Rusty mad. Four .404s for a Dall ram (he not carrying #2 gun or #3, cause who knows where grizzly might be?). If he needed four for the ram, maybe four times four for the bear.

More skinning, more packing, two great trophy heads, and a wait for the helicopter out servicing Tex and M.A.s Pete-Bill. They all had Dall ram that day. Five sets of horns held in the arms of five shit-eating grins standing in semicircle on the banks of Dolly Ding Bat Lake as the pictures were taken, and long careful discussions with Big Luke on taxidermy and where the Moe Henry and Obungekat Safari Group recommended the preservation of the head—any fifty-year guarantee outfits around, or century mounters? "There's no real craftsmen left," says M.A. Pete. "Just embalmers," said Tex.

Going for the grizzer wasn't nearly so good. Mr. Cop Turd, carrying Rusty, M.A. Bill, and Ollie, went flying by one pure grizzly standing out in an alpine meadow out on a flank of mountain where the spruce grew up in columns like the teeth of a comb and they had been swinging so good knocking down trophies that Rusty got Napoleonic, rode his luck all the way to Veneria and back, and made the pilot set them down two hundred meager yards away, which is to say he put Rusty out first at Rusty's demand, Rusty going down the winch, that two hundred yards' separation from the bear not very much when you're waiting for the guide and your rifle buddy to follow, but no choice, the alpine meadow was small, so there was Rusty on the ground alone unslinging his Jeffrey, all alone when the bear instead of deciding to meander away from the helicopter and the man, or take a long-distance look, came bearing instead into them with a roar—hours later D.J. could still hear it echoing out of the ashy pores of Rusty's monumentally shaken skin. Well, Mr. Cop Turd wasn't waiting for Rusty to down that grizzer standing in an alpine meadow all alone, no, they were not going to let any bear hang a human trophy in his den, not at the expense of the Moe Henry Group. Hail the Cop jammed his whirlybird right down on a line toward the bear charging so near overhead that the bear reached up with his paws and took a mighty swipe, at which point Rusty got a shot off, a decent shot, decent enough to miss the copter by as much as it missed the bear, and sound of the shot, Old Grizzer split ass for the woods, while Cop-bird whirlybird came back and picked up Old Rust—Old Zinc White ex Rusty Jethroe—even the shit hue in his eyes pale as junket, and back they went to the bunkhouse. Discussion that night. Rusty was sick. He had to get it up. They had to go for grizzer now. Well, he was man enough to steel his guts before necessity, he not D.J.'s father for naught tickle, D.J. was conceived in *deep* waters. So Rusty agreed in his own heart to get it up. Now he's awake, man, lying in his bunk looking out a small six-pane window at moonlight on the lake, and the smell of the pine grove around the bunkhouse is strong, it speaks of Indian caverns, of forest no white man ever saw, which is to say it smells like no pine forest Rusty ever saw, for the odor goes in and in again until he is afraid to breathe all the way, aisles are opening in his brain before the incense of it which is like the odor of the long fall in a dream. Blasts of rage and gouts of fear burn like jets and flush like bile waters and he is humped in his mind on Hallie, D.J.'s own father, Rusty, married twenty years to a blond beauty he can never own for certain in the flesh of his brain.

★

INTRO BEEP 7

★

Yeah, the time is soon coming, thinks Rusty, when fornication will be professional athletics, and everybody will watch the national eliminations on TV. Will boys like D.J. and Tex be in the finals with a couple of Playboy bunnies or black ass honeys? well, shit-and-sure, fifty thousand major league fuckers will be clawing and cutting to get in the big time to present their open flower petal pussy, or hand-hewn diamond tool and testicles in happy magnification by Color Vision RCA. Only thing holding this scheme back is the problems of integration. What if the Spades run away with the jewels? Not to mention all the wet pussy in America. Think of that in Color TV—all the purple majesty, hey says Rusty, if they do, America'll really be looking for a white hope, huh.

Of course, thinks Rusty, I'll be having to watch. Oh, the ignominy. Just stick my middle-age dick against the screen. Yeah, sighs Rusty, the twentieth century is breaking up the ball game, and Rusty thinks large common thoughts such as these: (1) The women are free. They fuck too many to believe one man can do the job. (2) The Niggers are free, and the dues they got to be paid is no Texas virgin's delight. (3) The Niggers and the women are fucking each other. (4) The Yellow races are breaking loose. (5) Africa is breaking loose. (6) The adolescents are breaking loose including his own son. (7) The European nations hate America's guts. (8) The products are no fucking good anymore. (9) Communism is a system guaranteed to collect dues from all losers. (9a) More losers than winners. (9b) and out: Communism is going to defeat capitalism, unless promptly destroyed. (10) a. Fucking is king. b. Jerk-off dances are the royal road to the fuck. c. Rusty no great jerk-off dancer. d. Rusty disqualified from playing King Fuck. (11) The white men are no longer champions in boxing. (12) The great white athlete is being superseded by the great black athlete. (13) The Jews run the Eastern wing of the Democratic party. (14) Karate, a Jap sport, is now prerequisite to good street fighting. (15) The sons of the working class

are running around America on motorcycles. (16)
Church is out, LSD is in. (17) He, Rusty, is fucked
unless he gets that bear, for if he don't, white men are
fucked more and they can take no more. Rusty's secret
is that he sees himself as one of the pillars of the
firmament, yeah, man—he reads the world's doom in
his own fuckup. If he is less great than God intended
him to be, then America is in Trouble. They don't
breed Texans for nothing. Rusty has a great philos-
ophy, states D.J., it is just you have to be an honest son
of a bitch to make it work, for—peer into this—you're
the fulcrum of the universe, right? the good Lord takes
his reading off you, right? (Rusty figures—D.J. will tell
you—that the Lord despising mass methods does not
bother to weigh man in the aggregate or the mass;
instead he stays close to a chosen few, and they ain't
Hebes, Rusty hopes to tell you) so Rusty being the cat
off whom the reading is read, being that fundament of
mind, flesh, and being whose moves are intimate to the
Lord, he got to be honest with himself if he want to be
on fulcrum point, because if he think he's doing good,
and the good Lord knows he's not, well, kiss your own
sweet ass, Eustachia, Rusty is then no longer up tight
with G.O.D.—Grand Old Divinity (biggest corporation of them all? Rusty often thinks not) no, you are
one place, God is another, how can you serve? But then
an asshole, even a H.G. asshole, cannot be honest by
definition, for it would claim to be an organ like any
other, it would pretend to have no guilt, and yet it
fumes, man. Ho, ho, wait and see.

★

CHAP SEVEN

★

Big Luke and Kenny Easterly were not running velvet guided tours of America's last unspoiled wilderness
for naught tickle either, so they decided to have the
whole group together on the grizzer hunt, five guests,
four guides, and Mr. Guide Pilot in Cop-Bird Seat, Al
Bell was his name flying a Bell 47J, three passengers,
one pilot—take a bow—Al Bell, no relation to Bell 47J.

Big Luke had a military decision. Whether due to
the atom bomb or to Al Bell and his 47J and numerous
other yclepts helicopts from Sam Sting Safari, and

other Safari Counters with their respective airplanes, Cop Turds, and general fission of the psychomagnetic field (new concept, Suck-Mouth) of the wild life in the Brooks Range, the fact is that the grizzers had gone ape. Big Luke had known grizzers all his life—there was a time when he knew them so well he could walk up to a peaceful one and pat him on the shoulder, the bear ain't an undivided heavy, a stone sadist, no, grizzer can be patted on the back, at least was a time but now the psychomagnetic field was a mosaic, a fragmented vase as Horace said to Ovid, and Big Luke couldn't be sure if he was still in contact with his monumental cool, too many grizzers were charging the hunter before the first shot. So Big Luke took a military fix. He had two adolescents who could shoot *maybe,* and one high-grade asshole who could shoot some of the time, and two M.A.s who had a fifty-fifty even locating a moving target in their scope. He had the guides of course, he could count on his guides, they would hold, they would keep shooting until the bear's breath was up their nose, but the clients had to get the first shot (with any pretense of class, the second as well) so look, here's a grizzer, wounded twice, a mind now halfway between dragon and dinosaur, fire in his gut, lightning in his shoulder, and zero in his life but heart, teeth, fangs, get those long claws in, and Luke's guide waiting for client to get two shots off now has the Grizzly Express running straight on them, not forty yards away, hop, lurch, leap, heave. For those forty yards the grizzer could be fast as a mustang. Even if guide hits him three times more, maybe grizzer doesn't stop until he takes a human trophy out with him into the twilight beyond the painted waters. "Ah swan," says Big Luke, "my client died in the old bear's arms." Shit! That cannot be. Big Luke has never lost a client, but there are averages, laws, and retribution. Cop Turds are exploding psychic ecology all over the place, and this is above the *Circle,* man, every mind, human, animal, even vegetable, certainly mineral (crystal mineral) is tuned in to the same place, wait and see, better believe, Big Luke knows he's getting away with too much, he's violating the divine economy which presides over hunters, and so he could lose a client, he would mar the record of a life, this is Yukon, man, heroes fall, listen to Big Luke folklore, Big Ruby Lil, the great whore of Saskatchewan, never failed to please a client, giants and pygmies they all came—Luke could tell the tale—until the day she pressed her luck, took Yukon hashish—what?—to speed the passing of the hours, and behold an auditor from Manitoba rolled in her comfortable soft brown slightly charred (from thirty years of peter burn) sweet whore's old Cadillac of a cunt, it was thus big and roomy (the secret was that her clients used to let the fatigue of a lifetime shoot, fire or seep out into those homey cunt walls—she was medicine, man) well, the audit got it up but he could not let it go, there was a knot of congested fatigue in his heart, he was afraid he would blast himself if he ever blew it into her, so Ruby Lil tried everything, she even, after four hours, sucked his dick, and Ruby Lil had not done that for twenty years, she was a Mexico-Eskimo Queen, man, she put down the taste of semen, but she even did the rim on that auditor with the eyeglasses from Manitoba, yet she failed, he never got the first drop to say sayonara to his dick, no floods of seed left the comptometer of his nuts, and Ruby Lil declined and was diminished to a dyke.

This Big Luke's thought? No, it's D.J. on the edge of masturbating in the Alaska night, with the excitement of going for griz in the morning, and holding off, holding off, cause a handful of spit on a sixteen-year-old dick puts a worm on the trigger and you slip off your shot.

This is defalcation from the point. Big Luke is also lying awake, and the knot of fatigue in the auditor from Manitoba's heart which D.J. is cooking via his fantasy is the actual knot of tired Herr Dread in Big Luke's heart (how's that for symbology, syph-head?). Yeah, now. So Big Luke General Fellinka makes his military disposition. They must be in position to bomb and superblast any grizzer who attacks. Therefore they will all make it together—five clients, five guides, Luke knows the spot, there's the bank of a mud-lick where berries grow—but the nightmare persists. Military solutions proliferate new problems, Pierrot. If General Luke has his double line of infantry, five clients in a straight row with five guides behind, just let one grizzer break through the line, and clients will be

shooting at each other and at guides, what embroil-
ment! no, the bank of the mud-lick is out, he'll have
to form a circle around a knoll, and pictures of terrain
circulate his head, revolve, come to a stop, start up
again.

Big Luke finally picked the patch. It was a chimney
of vertical rock round about one hundred feet in diameter, and bushes at its base where hunters could fire
from cover. It stood in the middle of one emerald
alpine meadow far enough beneath timber to hope and
expect for more than one or two bear, and patches of
buffalo berry and blueberry showed at the edge of the
trees. Luke disposed his Hot-Shot Special as follows:
ten men including himself set out in an arc one-third
of the way around the chimney on the side facing those
berry bushes (upwind side) and he pinned the line
with two guides at each end. Five hunters and himself
in the middle. By that method, the fire of two guides
would impact on any bear circling around the flank
from the blind side of the chimney, and the cross fire of
all four guides ready to concentrate on any one bear
attacking anywhere up the middle. If the bear ever
reached the center, Luke knew he there to be the man
to stop it. Thus disposition is done. General Luke
Fellinka now trundled the Pure Pores boys and Moe
Henry guides in by copter to a knoll one mile away
and then walked them over open country, high on the
ridgeline, so no bear could pop in on them in the
brushwood.

All set up, Big Luke made a speech. "Don't hold fire

too much! Any bear you see belongs to all of you. You can all shoot. That's the way to take him out." Shadow of Ruby Lil passes all unseen over Big Luke's brainpan.

"Who does the bear belong to?" asks Rusty.

"I'll know," said Big Luke. "I can tell if the first shot should get the credit, or if it belongs to a later shot when that's the one does the work."

Well, they didn't have too much to wait. Ninety minutes later, about eleven in the morning, two bears wandered into the meadow, husband and wife but for the lack of a J.P., and the wind came across the meadow from them sailing with such connubial grizzly funky strength that Tex swore afterward he could smell the bear on the breeze, and that was why he saw them first. Tex got off his shot first—it was his hunt this year—the male was dead with a .270 through the brain, and Rusty and Pete fired off two shots each at the other bear who let loose a roar like the explosion in the foghorn of a small-town firehouse when the noon alarm goes off. And then she turned and smashed off into the woods, blood all over her back and flank, and was hit eight more times by the guides, and dropped not ten yards back into the trees.

Big Luke gave the award to M.A. Pete. The second bear was Pete's bear, decided Luke. Pete was ready to give it all to Rusty, and his cannon too, but Luke after leading Rusty, Pete, Tex, and a couple of guides up to Tex's bear (proved to be stone dead on approach by failing any quiver when stones were tossed at him) now

walked on, rifle at the hip, following the trail of the
female whose blood was red on the alders and the
dwarf birch trees, blood looking to expire into brown
gum on the pine needles still bright as electric red on
the cedar leaves, that red vibrating up D.J.'s nose in
the cool gray blue ass sky green gray ground of North-
land, up above the Circle, red above the Circle, red in
the cool September Arctic air. Some giant wolf in
D.J.'s heart, some prehistoric wolf all eight feet big
began to stir new boils and springs and pools in the
river of D.J., in his blood, beasty audience, in his
blood, and he had to get him a wolf in the form of a
bear like the grizzly bear plugged with twelve shots
which lay there still shaking and broken and dead but
still twitching, that female bear her belly half demol-
ished by the Nitro Express of Medium Asshole Assistant to Procurement Manager Pure Pores Pete. Yeah.
Rusty's shot had broken the shoulder and probably
carried near the heart, but Pete got the duke. "I think
this bear went from massive shock," said Big Luke,
hardly able to hold back a massive shocker of a shit-
eating grin. "Yours was nice shooting, Rusty—" dig—
first time Luke calls Sir Jet-Throne, Rusty "—but Pete
did the real job, so I'd call it."

Pete began to think of moving to Kansas City. That
corporation land is mother, father, children, wife, hot
weekend fuck, and romantic sorrow all in one. There
are corporation execs who have sensibility fine as Anna
K.'s (Anna Karenina, hunk-head!) for one thing: their

boss. They know when their boss has ceased to love them. M.A.s in corporation land are vacuum tubes, man, ideal diodes, they are there to damp the waves in one direction, send them out the other, yes, yes, and cut out all the no no no. How else a boss to build up potential to transmit his communications without a M.A. vacuum tube or two in his network, Fergus? Well, the filament just burned out on Pete's tube. Ideal diode is no more.

"Where are you going to get that bear stuffed, Pete?" said Rusty.

"What do you recommend, Rusty?"

"Shoot another bear so you can patch the holes in this one."

What a cunt of a remark! But Rusty's got cunt in him. Vicious little streak he passed right on intact to D.J. Rusty don't look like Henry Cabot Lodge for nothing, he's already up and about and looking forward. Cause if he don't get a bear now, he can transfer to Japan.

Well, so there they go, right back to the chimney. And they wait for more bear. And more bear ain't coming. Bear may have gone ape shit in the Brooks Range, but they are not kamikaze, they can smell their own bear gum blood on the evergreen needles, and smell the insects strumming out all kinds of electronic ax music while insect pissing and shitting and orgy blood fucking with the flies in the wet red on the meadow and the woods, yeah, and those bears can

smell the last shit blasted out of dead female grizzer
with twelve slugs in her, and the shit that is ejected
after death has passed through the vale and got an odor
of the other, of the tomb, like the odor of cigarette
breath on the mouth of a bitch who smokes forty cigs a
day, you know the smell that goes back to Egypt. No
bear comes. Not all the rest of that day, and back again
in the morning, not all the rest of the next day. Next
day Tex and M.A. Pete go off with guides to look for
moose, Cop Turd is carrying them to a good shallow
moose lake, and Rusty and D.J. are left with M.A. Bill
and his Boom Boom Boomerang .311 Genius Special.
It's amazing what waiting can do to a man's guts. M.A.
Bill gets dreamy. He ceases to desire bear. Rusty scur-
ries about in his gut and reamasses his cool. He is
getting to feel taut and not without his ready—D.J. is
more so than a young assassin with a knife. He too has
got to get grizzer. The wolf is burning fever in him
now, best future of his blood is going to boil off if he
can't get on a bear (for he was the only one not to shoot
at the female grizzer) —he had (tell it not even to thine
own armpit) —he had blown up in bull buck bear
fever. Or maybe it was all that jack-off tension over
Ruby Lil, yeah. The scope had done a wiggle, finger
did the trigger in a jig and never pulled at all. So he is
in the heart of horror, he and Rusty can sit no longer
in the brush at the foot of the chimney looking at a lazy
meadow where no bear comes to feed on berries, and
the only sight in an hour is a loon winging on south

from high overhead. They could be as well out in
Texas desert as in this gray ass Arctic Circle with its
emerald green lawns and the itch-dick memory of electric red on the leaves. So they push on Luke to go out
tracking for bear, to push any direction into the wind
down trails through woods, fuck the cautions, Rusty is
indicating to Luke, let them be hunters at last and take
a trek for game. And Luke resists, just as long as he
can, he resists, for the word is out to the grizzers on the
Brooks Range, this piece of patch anyway—and there's
sullen babies inside those bear hides now, they could
make an Ace Delinquent on a bad Spade drunk seem
like Angel Enlightenment next to the look building in
those itty-bitty mean grizzer eyes. "Shit, man," said
Rusty finally, "I'm taking D.J. here and we are going
to walk all fifteen miles back to Ding Bat and see if we
can't encounter what we came to find." And Luke is
wishing he had given the hide to Rusty.

Well, naught tickle to fare, Big Luke radios Cop
Turd and tells him they're coming in on foot, and he'll
give him another toodle-oo in two hours forty, and
they string out now, Ed Smith the guide at point,
Rusty, D.J., M.A. Bill and Big Luke. D.J. is finally
walking with a gun across some miles of terrain in the
Endicott Mountains of the untapped last wilderness
Brooks Range.

And it's not that wild, man, it's not jungle, icicles,
glaciers, mountain peaks, abysses, no, man, this patch
right by to them here is nearly like Switzerland, but

stretched out, baby, hint of big stuff, frozen ass snow peaks to the north, howlers of wind in the big cavities of the big mountains, but here it's just as clear and clean as a tasty blond fuck, I mean D.J. could say you might just as well be in Yosemite, Evan, you can't beat this land for long big clean cool, evergreens, man, the odor of evergreens pervadeth.

But Rusty is half-insane by now. That odor of evergreen might just as well be poppers for his inflamed brain. He ain't trundling his ass for two hours forty in order for Big Luke to radio the Cop Turd and taxi them in, he's not there to have his lust blooded and placated, he is up, his guts are there. So he turns to D.J. and says, "Son, let's split from Luke the Fink cause he ain't going to get your ass or mine near a grizzer." And D.J. who has been feeling the high hairy cool of a terrible turn where your short will hold or not hold old bitch road, it's endless, yes, that moment has been riding the next moment every step of their walk, he don't know if he's going to be a hero or dead, but he loves his daddy this instant, what a fuck of a stud, they will take off together, they will make their own way back to Camp, and Big Luke will sweat a huge drop. So in a turn around a ledge in the woods, they bear off sharp right, climb the ledge, let the others pass beneath, and work fast in the other direction, running when they are out of sight. Maybe they have run up a distance of a half mile in the woods before Big Luke will be aware they are gone, and Big Luke will work a quarter-mile circle for an hour at least before he decides they have dumped him. At which point they will be two miles away, and Rusty thereupon sprints off with D.J., making real rough woodsman time through these woods, easy going, lots of carpet, very still, little animals scattering, Northern cool slowly settling. They are off on a free, father and son.

incest

★

――――――――

INTRO BEEP 8

――――――――

★

The pure moment of salt forming the crystal of this narrative going through D.J.'s super-accelerated consciousness at eighteen right here and now when he sitting at the dinner table in the Dallas ass manse with Mr. Rusty Smoking Jacket, Halleloo all beautiful perfumed tits popping big tasty hostess heaves and Tex across from him, D.J.'s mother humping up secret heart of pussy welter wallow and slide tug suck fuck for Tex's nineteen-year-old dick, Tex, D.J.'s best friend, blood brother, incest is electric man, never forget, and

eighteen between D.J. and Rusty it is all torn, all ties
of properly sublimated parental-filial libido have been
X-ed out man, die, love, die in a diode, cause love is
dialectic, man, back and forth, hate and sweet, leer-
love, spit-tickle, bite-lick, love is dialectic, and corporation is DC, direct current, diehard charge, no dialectic
man, just one-way street, they don't call it Washington
D.C. for nothing, eighteen, it's all torn, torn by the in-
exorable hunt logic of the Brooks Range when D.J.
was sixteen, wait and see. Here they go. Here is the
result of Rusty losing female grizzer with twelve male
plugs from I don't know how many shooting tubes,
think of fighting over a trophy which is as unknowing
of its killer as the poor town fuck must be unknowing
of the parental origins of her latest feet-ass (and head)
now in embryo in her womb, forgive D.J. for acting
like Dr. James Joyce, all junkies are the same, you
know. Follow the hunt.

★
─────────
─────────

CHAP EIGHT

─────────
─────────
★

Rust has been studying the map. He and D.J. are
map readers (at your service, coordinates) and compass hounds. He even bought D.J. a Keuffel & Esser
surveyor's transit, tripod, and tape for his fourteenth
birthday. He knows they now have eleven miles to
make before dark and five to six hours to do it in—
long twilight still, endless ass of ass-end summer long
Alaskan twilight, and he's not worried a bit at that,
he's free, man, loose, loose as Henry with a goose, shed-
ding those corporation layers, all that paper ass desk

shit and glut, dictating larynx ass machines, six-button Tphones, buzzer shit (conference table alcohol—where is your buzz), deadass hour shit, and he's free of Luke the Fink with his Washington up your ass connections, he's being bad Rusty and it's years, man, he wants to holler hallo for a grizzer any size big ass beast.

They go, putting on the miles, walking ten yards apart, crossing bare ridgelines when they feel they far enough away from Luke to take the chance, then ducking back to timber when they hear whirlybird Cop Turd glomming over the next hill, yeah, Luke has put in a call, round up those strays, shit, no one is going to round them up. And after an hour, a good sweat on each, father and son sweat, a little alike, a little diff, Rusty got just a hint of sweet rot in his smell but when the balls is back in as now he's okay, many a hero smell worse than old Rust, and they go like two combat wolves, eyes to the left, eyes to the right, slow relaxed sweep, looking, listening to the *mood,* man, their steps keen off each little start of sound, squirrels on a split ass, working upwind through the timber, skirting all the alder, briers, snag-brush, working their way into the wind as if they going to *smell* that bear. And when they stop to rest, they are real good, man, tight as combat buddies, they pick a spot under an overhang rock at their back so no bear can come up behind and the touch, just the feather on your ass touch, of danger, cause grizzer could be anywhere near, is ozone bubble in the nose, that oo oo oo of the nose when you going to meet a real hot fuck in an hour and you know she there waiting for you, whoo-ee, whoo-ee, humping a sweet pump by the railroad track beautiful big-ass Texas night. Rusty starts to talk. They looking out off a ledge onto a view of stone ice peaks twenty miles away, could be Colorado, not Alaska in September, and those mountains full of evergreen dropping in long fat sweet ass sweet husband fat-ass type of lines, the rolling stands of evergreen looking like fur on the ass of the grizzer, yeah, those soft humps of mountains are like sleeping bears, big haunches of hibernation, Hiram, and Rusty starts to point out the local flora, the tall saxifrages like the boykinia, the sowdock, fireweed, horsetail, he been pointing them out all along as they were going, just a quiet little voice, "That's white bell of heather over there, D.J." or "Hot damn, look at the height of those horsetails," "White mountain avens, boy, pretty flower that," "Purple rhododendrons, up in the Circle! Wait till I tell your mother I saw purple rhododendrons in the Arctic Circle." Oh, there's cow parsnip and climbing bells, yellow arctic poppies, more of a fine white little flower he calls saxifrage again. "Know what saxifrage means, kid?"

"You tell me."

"Rock buster. That little white flower is a rock buster. Any saxifrage is strong enough to grow and split a rock." And D.J. reels with that, cause he thinks of the little green shoot (or is it white? underground, just nipple tit out of the seed) getting its white nose into the smallest crack of the rock and pushing and the rock pushing back, and it swelling to crack the rock. and the rock not cracking, how can a soft shoot move rock? Yeah, well it sends out the word to the root and the root pulls into the basic ass power of the earth and draws a force, a subterranean thunder, Wanda, and womb, woom woom woom, one little blast of swell, that shoot is harder than rock for one micromillionth of a second, it got a hard on, Herbert, and the rock stone pussy cracks, and up comes boykinia the local saxifrage. Just rock buster. D.J. is humper-ding with sweet pores of thought. Damn.

"That's monkshood," says Rusty.

About then was when they first sat looking out across a canyon and a long field of tundra turning red and yellow already and a pioneer tree in the middle of it.

"Man, you like to be a tree by yourself in the middle of a field?" asks Rusty.

"Now you know I really don't know," says D.J. confessing ignorance for the first time since thirteen.

"My grandmammy, your great-grandmother Eula Spicer Jethroe, used to be a witch, so evehbody claims. She used to tell me when I was a little three-year-old still shit ass in my breeches that I must never sleep under a pioneer tree, cause it is full of sorrow and alone and bats piss on it at midnight, therefore it stands by itself getting messages, all kind of special messages, and if you sleep under it, you witched by it, you get the messages too."

"What are they?"

"I don't know. Old Eula Spicer Jethroe wouldn't say." Yeah, they laughed. D.J. said, oh, cautious as they come, "Rusty . . . sir . . . how do you know the names of all this grass . . . herb . . . all this."

"Why I spent a half hour talking to Luke asking the names. That's the only good half hour I had with him. Cause that used to be my hobby. When I was your age I used to be a walking compendium of Texas wild flowers."

"Say, you never let on."

"Well, D.J., my daddy had more time, you know. Him and me were close, you know cause it was all that time, depression, East Texas depression years, cold heart times. He had no work so we went hunting for meat. Then two years later he hit a well and the Jethroes was rich again, but those two years I saw sights, learned things. We used to camp out in a lean-to right on the plains. Coyotes. Oh, that's a cry."

"I've heard it hunting."

"Yeah, but in a lean-to set up so the rain don't blow in the open end, and starting a fire in the rain, know how to do that?"

"No, sir."

"Well, you got to look for a stump that's protected by overhang, or the underside of a tree branch that's rotten, you got to find dry punk, that dry perfumy sort of rot stuff in a tree, and that's your tinder and your paper all in one. If it's dry, it will get wet twigs to burn. So, that we used to do, daddy and me, used to camp out there four days in a row, trailing across that plain till an animal got in range, not so easy when the plain is bare, you hear, and we had to make the shots count too, I learned a lot from my daddy, he taught me one thing I'm going to teach you now—the only time a good man with a good rifle is in trouble is when he steps from sunlight into shadow, cause there's two or three seconds when you can't see."

"I know that, daddy," says D.J.

"Yeah, but you never made a principle of it. That's the difference."

"Yessir, yessir."

"Listen, know the worst thing I ever saw. It was a poor deer being killed by an eagle. Some hunter had wounded the deer—the eagle finished the job or was about to when I couldn't stand to watch no more and shot the eagle and put the poor deer out of its miz. But that eagle had swooped in, plucked out one eye of the deer, fluttered up a little you know like a Nigger strutting his ass feathers, and then plucked the other eye. It was going to go for the nuts next. Terrible creature the eagle. I've heard they even pull the intestine out of a carcass like a sailor pulling rope with his mouth. It got me so upset to recognize that E Pluribus Unum is in the hands of an eagle that I almost wrote an open letter to the Congress of America. Can you imagine your daddy getting that ape shit? But I think it's a secret crime that America, which is the greatest nation ever lived, better read a lot of history to see how shit-and-sure a proposition that is, is nonetheless repre-sented, indeed even symbolized by an eagle, the most miserable of the scavengers, worse than crow."

On and on they go for half an hour, talking so close that D.J. can even get familiar with Rusty's breath which is all right. It got a hint of middle-aged fatigue of twenty years of doing all the little things body did not want to do, that flat sour of the slightly used up, and there's a hint of garlic or onion, and tobacco, and twenty years of booze gives a little permanent rot to the odor coming off the lining of the stomach, and there's even a speck of caries, one bit of dental rot almost on the agreeable side (for face it, fellow Ameri-cans, there are secret freaked-out grope types who dig dental rot if its subtle kind of high clean funky smell, how often, after all, does a nose get near a living nerve?) but with all this detraction, fatigue, booze, Nick the Teen, garlic and cavity, it's still a good breath, it got muscle and a big happy man with that clean odorless white American flesh (hey assholes out there, is this D.J. addressing you a Texas youth for sure or is he a genius of a crippled Spade up in Harlem making all this shit up, better wonder, work your bronze, this is a problem—whose consciousness you getting, overlap on the frequencies, Percival? shit, D.J. is going to make you fly up your own ass before you get to read him right, it's love to have the consciousness of D.J., Texas youth, better believe, cause it's easier for

D.J. to imitate a high I.Q. Harlem Nigger time to time, since D.J. knows New York, yeah, he passed through, MacDougal Street you wait and see, than for a Harlem Nigger ever to know all this secret Texas shit. Well, place your bets, worry your head audience of D.J. (there is no security in this consciousness,) and you are going to die some day and there is no security in that, well, before you buy your casket Mr. Rot Gut wait till you get to know Tex and his own daddy Gottfried Hyde Senior, the undertaker, there's a piece of woo, and point coming here, point your nose, auditor, is that D.J. riding on currents of love can take all the smell of his daddy's breath and love him still, cause that's love—you can go to the end of the other's breath and still forgive him. If you husbands and wives out there in receiving land cannot do that, well, hump your shrug, all is not hopeless, maybe you still in love if only with limp dick and just one lip of the pussy, or two lips of cunt dry as adhesive tape. Whoo-ee!) D.J. takes his consciousness and by act of will zooms with Superman moves of his brain projectile back to ledge, back to rock, and Rusty pointing across the valley to a caribou upwind from them, a caribou just standing near the pioneer tree, and Rusty lifts his rifle, breathes, waits to feel D.J.'s mood, waits, puts down his rifle. "Shall we let it go?"

"Yeah."

"Yeah, son. Shit, let's let old caribou go. He suffering anyway."

And that old caribou is standing with his nose in the moss, digging his nose in, and his haunches are hicking and twitching and his stump tail is wiggling like a baby's running nose. Alaska flies are murdering him, he stands, suffers, then makes a dash for two hundred yards to escape the flies, stands, looks for damp in the tundra, holds it, suffers the flies, then runs again, on up to the ridge where there will be wind maybe, maybe there will be wind, and he can clear his head from thirty fly bite on the minute. And Rusty and D.J. watching have been waiting for fifteen minutes, and there's fine cool in them now, they're off the fever of hunting and into the heart of it, the cool, letting that caribou go has got them so ready for bear they could believe in man-bear radar, it's as if now they know, cause the pitch of secret tune is pure that grizzer is near, something big is by. And as they step out, they have not gone one-half of a mile before they find a track, fresh bear track on the wet earth of a high mountain rivulet, and their hearts hold, cause track is big, Rusty could put the soles of both his big hunting shoes inside that one bear's foot, and mark of the claws in front is long, two inches long of claws, this is grizzer, grizzer baby, never black bear, not with claws two inches long. Now they feel the size. They've been thinking of grizzer as a big big man, about as frighten-ing as a stone-black seven-foot three-hundred-pound Nigger, but grizzer is bigger than that, grizzer is right up there with the hippopotami and the small elephants, and the big elephants, yeah, that's how it feels, now they feel alone and in the woods with some fast dark boxcar size of beast moving somewhere around in relation to them. Shit! And the Cop Turd comes by overhead shaking the silence, and failing to see them in the woods, and Rusty says in a hoarse little clearing of his throat (just like a little clearing in the forest) "Hey, now, D.J., we're on bear traveling trail." And through the brush ahead is a path, looks like it's been grooved by many a grizzer working down the same route through the brush, and there and here, bark rubbed from trees, familiar intimate family rub of itching hide and itching bear asshole rubbing against that old corncob bark. Yeah, some nappy mountain of grizzly has been lumbering and slinging his legs along here. And D.J. breathes death—first time in his life—and the sides of the trail slam onto his heart like the jaws of a vise cause that grizzer could come erupting out of the brush, could a grizzer travel at speed through that brush? it's death D.J.'s breathing, it comes like attack of vertigo when stepping into dark and smelling pig shit, that's what death smells to him, own pig shit smell, terrible fear right out of his lungs and pores, mucous lining of now flappy-ass organs, and back of fear like man riding chariot pulled by eight wild pigs in harness is crazy-ass murder, cause D.J. for first time in his life is hip to the hole of his center which is slippery desire to turn his gun and blast a shot into Rusty's fat fuck face, thump in his skull, whawng!

and whoong! with the dead-ass butt of his Remington 721, D.J. is shivering on the death in this hot-ass vale of breath, cause each near-silent step of his toe on the tail sounds a note, chimes of memory, angel's harp of ten little toes picking out the blows of Rusty's belt on his back, he five years old and shrieking off the fuck of his head, cause the face of his father is a madman ass, a power which wishes to beat him to death—for what no longer known—a child's screaming in the middle of, and so interrupting, a Hallelujah Sir Jet Throne fuck? nobody know now, D.J. just remembers the beating, screaming, pleading, smell of pig shit in his five-year-old pants, and death, coming in like oscillations red and green waves pulsating from oscilloscope, murder came red and green, stop, go, Rusty's eyes in to kill on D.J.—fat five-year-old spoiled beautiful little fuck in the middle between husband and wife, hola, Olatunji, vale of breath on the vise in his heart and first seed of tumor, figure-toi, could that be?—little pretty seed of backed-up murder passed from valve asshole Rusty's heart to the seat of D.J.'s brain, for Hallie rushed in then, picked up decanter whiskey, flung it through on a line through window, and glass crackled all scythe and lightnings, and spell broke, murder weather cracked in thunder, and D.J. all pig shit smell and five-year-old ass and back burning like the flesh in the burns of Hell run all screaming into Hallie's arms, little man saved by cunt, virility grew with a taint in the armature of the phallic catapult, call it tumor if that's what D.J.'s got in his brain, cause brilliance is next to murder, man, brilliance is green and gold light on the body and wings of horseflies hovering over the rot and gray-gold and red of degenerating meat. Whoo! Death is on him, memory of father near to murdering the son, breath of his own murder still running in the blood of his fingers, his hands, all murder held back, and then on the trail came a presence, no longer the fear of death but concentration, murder between the two men came to rest, for murder was outside them now, same murder which had been beaming in to D.J. while he thinking of murdering his father, the two men turned to contemplate the beast. Which was there? There before! No. Nothing to be seen. All calm now, as if they walking into the flat ass calm of a flat still sea, stepping in deeper on every step, their bodies in different states of immersion every breath, the late sun throwing out orange-lavender, and lead of color near to immersions now infusions of purple in deep of the wood, and each step took them into different domain, for D.J.'s nose was like a king surveying the principalities of the realm, bleed you not, Sigismunde, calm to calm they stepped on in along the trail, each step a rock God laid on water, hot horseshit Hercules, and hum the smells in that wood, Prince of Pals, they took one step through a kingdom of pines, mad genius pine trees, prescribing their aromatic antiseptic prescription for all things, incense saying come to me I am all, I am siren of the North,

nerve of the Arctic Circle with affiliates down to the
Equator, I'm a brain, man, pine needles my calling
card.

Next step, in they're plunged into some rot, some
stump of dwarf birch, bark rubbed ass of raw by tail of
bear or moose of caribou antlers eight years ago! like
that! and dying over the years, cause a ring of bark had
been cut and the skin of such dying tree go to rot
beneath the trunk, fell down. Into the open mouth of
that remaining stump came the years of snow, sun,
little jewels of bird shit, cries of sap from the long
dying roots, the monomaniacal electric yodeling of
insects, and wood rotting into rotting wood, into ges-
tures of wood, into powder and punk all wet and
stinking with fracture between earth and sky, yeah,
D.J. could smell the break, gangrene in the wood,
electric rot cleaner than meat and sick shit smell and
red-hot blood of your flesh in putrefaction, but a con-
firmed wood gangrene nonetheless, Burbank, a chaos
of odor on the banks of the wound, nothing smells
worse than half-life, life which has no life but don't
know it—thank you, Mr. Philosopher, just show me
the hemorrhoids of the academy, and on that rock!
. . . Next step was into a pool of odor which came
from the sweets of the earth, sweet earth smell speaking
of endless noncontemplative powers, beds of rest, bur-
geonings, spring of life, a nectar for the man's muscles
on the odor of that breath, yeah, D.J. was breathing his
last, he was in the vale of breath, every small smell

counted, it was the most fucking delicious moment of his life up to that point, for there are those who know and those who do not know when a very bad grizz is near to you (a final division of humanity) and D.J. knew, and D.J. was in love with himself because he did not wish to scream or plead, he just wished to en-counter Mr. D., big-ass grizz, and the next step put his nose into an aisle of forest scents, herbs offering each their high priest of here, here is the secret lore and the cold fires of the temple, and leaf mold, wet molderings, some kind of forest good-bye weeded in from the mes-sages of the wind, sending back to the peasant, back to the farm, then moss, new greenings, the odor of forest beginnings like baby ass powder and tiny flowers, the tenderness of the tip where life began, and some sweet wine of old funk in the moss as well, some odor of dwarf's armpits wiped with velvet, thank you, milady. That was when the grizz came.

Around a turn in the trail, by the side of a ledge, he'd been waiting, listening to the tick snap and twig crack of their boots, and he came at them from thirty yards away with the roar of nothing D.J. ever heard, like a foghorn fire siren about to burst, cause some congested hell in a whirlwind has come thundering with rocks down a hill out of its foghorn throat and D.J. heard the crazy wild ass moan of every animal they'd gunned down and the tear and blast of all flesh from all fat exploding knockout Magnums, what a cry came out of that shit ass beast, and frozen like prisoners in the searchlight, hypnotized half up to sky, and the air shivered as if a .105 howitzer just gone off, the grizzer came at them on the heuuuuuu of the cry, two red coal little eyes of fire, wall of fur coming fast as a locomotive barreling on that trail, and D.J. in some sweet cool of rest below all panic and paralysis dropped to one knee, threw up Remington, had a sail of light at the top of his head of far-gone tree and sky, and pulled off the trigger to smash a shot into that wall of fur, almost leisurely, like shot-putting a rock into a barrel, his eye not even to the scope, you could not miss if your arm had the strength to get the gun up. And Rusty fired from behind and that animal didn't stop, it kept coming on down like a twelve-foot surf of comber bamming right for your head, and D.J.'s heart and his soul sweet angel bird went up the elevator of his body and all balls but flew out before he slammed bolt and fired again at grizzer not ten yards away flame of the muzzle meeting flame from grizzer's red flame ass red mouth, grizzer kerwhonked half in air from the blast, took leap, hop, howl, one mad bound off trail, leaving a wake of hot caves, gamy earth, fur went by so near, yeah, one flash of blood on his honey hide, and then he went booming down the mean crazy slope of the ledge, twisting D.J.'s neck, so fast was the move. Then grizzer was gone.

Well, now they had a pretty, didn't they? How sweet seemed Big Luke's precaution stay in open with the bear. Now they had to climb down that fucking ledge

and somewhere down, down there in all that thicket
and brush and owl shit slunk and precipitous slope was
Mr. D., the Red Ball Express, half-dead or not nearly
dead at all, awful bad. They are doing their best not to
chatter, cackle, or carry on like birdwomen now.
"Never heard of a grizzer charging like that," said
Rusty's voice, weak as piss over pebbles.

"They gone ape shit just as Big Luke say." Hoarse
adolescent big phlegm voice.

"Yeah." Humps.

"Yeah." Humps. Echo in the silences.

"I wish I had my Ruger right now," said Rusty, big-
ass State Trooper style. "A rifle's too slow for tight-ass
quarters."

"Was you going to bring it?"

"I almost took it up from Ding Bat today."

The Ruger 44 Magnum is Rusty's twelve-inch
barrel pistol, detachable stock, comes highly recommended for bear in the brush. "That fucking Luke,"
says Rusty, "sticking us around the chimney—who's to
know we'd end up here?"

They are waiting for the other to be first to say, "Let
us go back to camp and come out tomorrow with the
Ruger and the mob." But they can't, and the moment
they are silent, echo of the event opens silence after
silence—they are close to puking they are so scared.
D.J. feels shit yellow between his toes, his bowels slosh
internal bilge, every bit of hard shit in him has broken
down to squirts like spit and dishwater rumblings. A

pall is on the woods. He can smell nothing but randy
ammonia in his armpits. Yeah. And like lightning
which cut across the sleeper's bed so close that sleeper
was turned and flung to the floor, so the memory of
Mr. D. (D for Death) Grizzer's mad-ball charge is like a
stroke across the strings of nerve in his life—say, it will
come back and back again.

Yeah, recollected in memory, it comes back to D.J.
eating in the Dallas ass manse, and he shivers—no man
cell in him can now forget that if the center of things is
insane, it is insane with force, heuuuuuu goes the
bellow of the grizzer in the salt on his meat and sorrow.
But bearable. Cause they went down for the grizzer
after all—here is how—58% of D.J. wanted nothing
but to leave Mr. Wounded Grizzer and get the fuck
out, in fact that 58% was pulling on his liver and
gut. But D.J. is a head man. Which is not to say he
gives head, but is ruled by his head. A creature of will.
That will now says to sixteen-year-old flesh, "Go back
without looking for this griz and Tex will ride your
ass to shit."

That's it. D.J. face the anger of God before he look
into the contempt and contumely of that State of
Texas personified by Gottfried Tex Hyde Jr. Whooee.

"Well, dad, let's start down after the animal."

"Right, son," and Rusty smiles with lips like two wet
soda crackers flapping at each other.

And the grizz is there. Forty shit-eating minutes
later, their backs wet, legs trembling like horse just run

the mile and a quarter, their hands slippery with coward oil (clam juice and sweat, you bird watcher) faces scratched like two bitches been working them over with *long* nails, lad, rifle stocks scratched, their knees, thighs, ribs and butts a congregate of bruises (which congregate is the established plural for bruises, look it up, turd pedant) their lungs fired from fear, funk, exhaustion and the anticipation that each step could back them into a wound-ass grizzer, they worked their collective father and son ass down the steep slope below the edge, farting through catbrier brush, dwarf alder brush, blueberry cranberry brush, rocks, slick-ass rocks, sharp-ass rocks to cut their hands, ghost trees with roots half-exposed on the near precipices of the slope, trees taking on witches' arms for shapes, limbs beseeching the North—O, power above the Circle, incantations and greetings from this witches' tree.

Well, they went down one at a time following a trail of blood as thick and clean as Sherwin-Williams Red. D.J. would go first and Randy would cover him— combat men flushing out a sniper. Then Randy would make his trip and pass D.J., D.J. meanwhile scanning about him in a 360 degree circle which meant thirty feet of visibility here, one hundred there, and wonder. Cause the blood led down and down, as if Mr. D., his insides a rocket of exploded works, was plunging like a cannonball to the bottom of something, and yet. All grizzers crazy. What if Mr. D. went down and then circled up to take them from behind? So D.J. scanned three hundred and sixty degrees about, waited till Rusty beckoned from below and then started his scratch-ass descent on the trail of the griz, passing Rusty with the high hard sobs of lungs working too hard, and Rusty sobbing back. What a fucking dual coward-ass twin sweat and sob that was. Wham! That Texas will carries Texas cowards to places they never dreamed of being. Vava, va va voom!

After forty minutes they made rendezvous. The griz was lying in a beat-down circle of brush which he must have tromped out forty or fifty times while going through one of the bends of his wounds, and he had set down like a tabby cat on its stomach, forelegs tucked under him, peaceful, looking to be stuffed bear served on a red plate ten feet in diameter, for that blood beneath was monumental in its pool. They came on him from a hundred feet above, and Rusty was for pouring in some lead just to make shit-and-sure, but peace was coming off that bear—it was like the moment a gull sets on water—and so Rusty contented himself—being a camera-conscious flash-bulb poking American—to heist a little stone and bap that bear on the hide. Old Griz raised its head a little. Not dead yet. And its mouth looked to laugh as if between the millstones of two huge pains (or was it three huge gears from three huge wounds?) something very funny has occurred, as if he was saying, "You put your palm sweat on that stone, mother-fucker, and I'm taking your sweat with me."

Rusty raised his gun, but D.J. touched the rifle slightly with a little salute, and started walking down toward the bear.

"Come back," Rusty whispered, "you're out of your fucking head," for D.J. was holding his rifle in one hand swinging down around his thigh. "You cover me, daddy," said D.J. to avoid a fishwife family gone-for-gooney while that poor huge beast was going. D.J. just had to see him up close.

At twenty feet away, D.J.'s little cool began to evaporate. Yeah, that beast was huge and then huge again, and he was still alive—his eyes looked right at D.J.'s like wise old gorilla eyes, and then they turned gold brown and red like the sky seen through a ruby crystal ball, eyes were transparent, and D.J. looked in from his twenty feet away and took a step and took another step and another step and something in that grizzer's eyes locked into his, a message, fellow, an intelligence of something very fine and very far away, just about as intelligent and wicked and merry as any sharp light D.J. had ever seen in any Texan's eyes any time (or overseas around the world) those eyes were telling him something, singeing him, branding some part of D.J.'s future, and then the reflection of a shattering message from the shattered internal organs of that bear came twisting through his eyes in a gale of pain, and the head went up, and the bear now too weak to stand up, the jaws worked the pain.

Then the gale subsided. The peace came back to the

eye, pain fading like the echo of the last good note, and that wild wicked little look of intelligence in the eye, saying something like, "Baby, you haven't begun," and when D.J. smiled, the eyes reacted, they shifted, they looked like they were about to slide off the last face of this presence, they looked to be drawing in the peace of the forest preserved for all animals as they die, the unspoken cool on tap in the veins of every tree, yes, griz was drawing in some music of the unheard burial march, and Rusty—wetting his pants, doubtless, from the excessive tension—chose that moment to shoot, and griz went up to death in one last paroxysm, legs thrashing, brain exploding from new galvanizings and overloadings of massive damage report, and one last final heuuuuuu, all forgiveness gone. And coughed blood out of his throat as he died.

D.J. didn't speak to Rusty on the way back. And when they hit camp at dark, Big Luke so relieved he couldn't even read various prescribed riot acts, they asked at last who had got the bear, and D.J., in the silence which followed, said, "Well, we both sent shots home, but I reckon Rusty got it," and Rusty didn't contradict him—one more long silence—and Rusty said, "Yeah, I guess it's mine, but one of its sweet legs belongs to D.J." Whew. Final end of love of one son for one father.

Next morning, crack ass of dawn, Rusty was overseeing the transfer of that dead and now dressed grizzer from his dried blood patch up the winch to the helicopter. And they figured the bear in his natural state had stood nine hundred pounds and more counting the claws.

★
_____

INTRO BEEP 9

_____
★

The hunting over? This fine narrative of native Texas pluck and grits now to be laid back into its rifle case while D.J.'s mind opens up another box of strict inside goodies? Screw. The climax within Alaska is yet to come—you will get rocks off you thought were buried forever. But rest for an inst. Return to civ, which is to say syphilization and/fuck/James Joyce—now enter D.J.'s genius head working its ventral hatch and vale, which is to say his *mouth,* turd nugget! at the dinner cited before in the Dallas ass manse, D.J. eighteen,

Incest
_cellardoor

two years later, composing in his head (while smiling at Texas tooth and cunt hostess types to right and left of him) —reach for your brains, Mr. Intellectual Testicles—let us snap down deep into D.J.'s mind patterns, and see if we pick up a universal mandolin or two, spelled mandala, dear Major Galliana, frostbite and fuck hairs, there is no logic to projects but incest, family bugger—you want to see D.J. the brain? he is working out the secret inner logic of piss. Now D.J. is a shit-oriented late adolescent, he is marooned, in case you have not noticed, on that balmy tropical isle pronounced Selador, spelled cellardoor—asshole—do you know a committee of Language Hump-type professors put out a committee finding back in 1936—most beautiful word in the English language is cellardoor. Think of that. The Isle of Selador—think of that. The Isle of Selador—otherwise known as cellardoor, the entrance to your asshole. Where we began was with fact one— D.J. is marooned on the balmy tropical isle of Anal Referent Metaphor. Now that's a moniker, man. You can see the fellow stand up and walk around, Anal Referent Metaphor! He's confidential secretary to America's #1 financial wizard Mr. Isower Anal Compulsive. You can write a fucking play suitable for staged readings about the confidential dialogue between the two. As viz:

Isower Anal Compulsive—How was your movement, today, Referent Metaphor?

Anal Referent Metaphor—Loose and slicky ass, Isower. How was yours?

I.A.C.—Bonded. We got to move some capital down the list.

A.R.M.—Set up a technical slide?

I.A.C.—For shit-and-sure, Señor Manure.

That's how they talk in the East, up in those bone Yankee ass Jew circumcised prick Wall Street palaces —take it from D.J.—he got psychic transistors in his ear (one more gift of the dying griz) which wingding on all-out pickup each set of transcontinental dialogues from the hearts of the prissy-assed and the prigged. Fungatz, radatz, and back to piss.

What can D.J. have to say about piss which is new? Whoo whoo. Piss, pious pretender, is a nerve of the wind when it's drilled from a peter. Rushings of the air, balms of the limbs (which is what air is, sexy). Piss, fascinated auditor of D.J.'s intellectual shuttlings and switchings, is a lullaby of the waters when it poozles from a sweet damp pussy. So get your turns recorded. Problem of piss broken down into two. Peter piss and cunt piss. Phallic urine, Vaginal urine. You're dealing with different details, Delilah, P.U. and V.U.

Well, this is deep stuff. Excrement is defeat. Liquid excrement otherwise known as You're-In Spa-ce-man is the defeat which comes from stand-up ventures where you had to wait. Someone talking, and you want to interrupt but you hold your tongue—that makes for piss. Gather near, D.J. tell you why. An impulse once it is frustrated crystallizes the chemicals which had been interacting in order to fuel the move. Why? Say, son, take something on faith. D.J. genius philosopher and commo engineer (that's communications, not Come-you-nism, Senator, although it's a mistake any intelligent Southerner might make) D.J., Grand Synthesizer of the Modern Void, suggests that the intellectual equipment to comprehend why frustration makes crystals of impulse when they are in the mode of liquid chemical matter is not yet yours. Study basic electricity, basic electronics. Come back. D.J. will stick an electrode up your ass. Now consider, take it on faith: a crystal is a receiving apparatus to draw in messages, because it's a form, man, a crystal is the most acute kind of form and forms are receptors of that which is less formed because that which is less formed looks to define itself by getting fucked by a form. You hip? That's why beauty stands still and lets a piece of ass come to it. Cause beauty is a high form. It is a crystal. It is the frustrated impulse of a general desire to improve the creation. So it fixed, man. How else comprehend the flowers? They get all the messages. Ever heard of a flower coming to you? Only its scent. But avoid complexities and reversals of direction at this stage—do not try to solve positive and negative electricity, rather gather on D.J.'s observed fact: frustration makes you telepathic, cause the cat's whisker (which is the frustrated nerve still dangling from the residue of the frustration) tickles that new-formed crystal of the impulse till the electronic message comes in. Frustration makes you more telepathic because it makes you more electric. Up to a point, Poindexter, after that, dielectric, apathetic, insulated, you ass. Cause to be telepathic while frustrated is to be burned on charged wire. After the bomb comes apathy. So call for the flushing waters. Your body, D.J. would inform you, sends out a call to all cell waters: gather here, kiss this crystal, dissolve its form. <u>Unloose my stasis</u>. Crystal washes down to glub, glub, glub. Urine is a pipe running the dissolution of all unheard messages. That's why people piss like horses at good parties and bad—they are getting uncouth oceanic messages from all over the room: come here, I want to fuck you; go there, I want to kill you. Whoo-ee! That bladder gets full of piss. Therefore, D.J. seeks to avoid all frustration of impulse in order to test his hypothesis. For figure thee, Henry, if D.J. makes it through a day without a single impulse held back, he should not need to piss a drop. That's science, dear clients.

★

CHAP NINE

★

At the party in Dallas ass manse, D.J. and Tex have each lined up the possible tooth and cunt hostesses they can fuck. That is simple. Some tooth and cunt hostesses are closet fucks. Walk in on them in an unlocked bathroom and you can have a two minute red-hot steaming ass blubber wet slap-dizzy oceanic cunt fuck. Need never fuck them again, understood, or don't fuck them again for six months. You just taking two minutes out of the tissue of responsible executive country club station wagon et cetera shit et cetera shit life.

de Sade

Key to it all, cause not all do, is don't make a mistake, adolescents! with the wrong kind of tooth and cunt responsible hostess type or she'll kick your nuts in: you got to pick the one with the right schizophrenia, that beam in the eye, that gleam of the mind which says I keep a closet for occasions, meet you on the moon for a sixty-second suck. Well, when fucking these mad insane ones, D.J. here to advise, get in fast, get out fast, cause they greedy fiends. This ain't young cunt from which you cop the goods—this is used cunt, burnt meat, cliff-hanging menopause types which can't get rid of the poisons by any hole but the pussy hole. They greedy fucking fiends. You accept their invitation on leaving the bathroom to make it with them in a motel and they get more out of you in three hours than a new chick emanating happy fucks would elicit in a day and a night. And the tooth and cunters are converting their schizophrenia into cancer juice for you. This too deep and disagreeable? Listen, loves, we getting back to Alaska soon, but Tex and D.J. for present period in their eighteen- and nineteen-year-old life are super-hot business cause they got illicits going, nobody like Tex and D.J., wait'll you hear.

They also on freak activities. Not just fucking two or three forty-year-old women on separate shots in the bathroom in one night, after all that's nothing once you read the Marquis de Sade, but they off on real freaks. For instance, they are digging corpses in Tex's father's funeral parlor, I don't mean the ultimate, the

156

boys are never without some kind of jammed-up taste and principles but listen city slickers from the East, they are engaging in private autopsies, undercover undertaker surgical activities—this weird unpalatable action to be explained on the basis that it gives them powers. They are not hunter-fighter-fuckers for nothing, no, nor with enclaves of high ability in karate, football, sports car, motorcycle, surfboard, and certain notions of the dance, as well as genius inquiries in electronics and applied existentialism without having to snoop here and there for powers, which they get from crime, closet fucking, potential overturn of incest since Tex is almost not above trying to get Hallie Jethroe in one closet fuck this very night, plus ghoul surgery on corpses which is demonological you may be shit-and-sure, and derives from their encounter with all the human shit and natural depth of their Moe Henry hunt two year ago.

So back to Alaska where the boys got their power. And they got them all Alaska style, as weird and wild-ass as the entrails of a wild-ass goose, just listen to this: D.J. was in such a murder ball of sick disgusted piss-on-dad after Rusty took claim of the bear that he couldn't sleep for fear he'd somnambulate long enough to beat in Rusty's head, so up he got, tapped Tex in his bunk, wide-awake as well, and in one whispered minute they decided to split and make a little trek right that night into Endicott Range. And that's where they are now (in D.J.'s mind two years later) right out in those hills

Maxwell's demon

eight miles already from Dolly Ding Bat, packboards carrying tent-cloths, grub, rifles, blankets, man they made their packs in the dark without waking Big Luke, Al Bell, Ollie, Rusty, or the medium assholes (who are all sleeping sound as slaughtered cattle) and off they go, taking the trail up the mountain, staying to the trail till dawn which is like four in the morning this part of September after the long Arctic twilight night of June and July and the very short night of August, so now the weather getting ready to take the dip into winter, they are working on the last of the early dawns.

It's hours before they speak, just working along in the early fall nip cold of the August night, breathing in hint of the chill of the frozen steam and the icy vise of magnetic north—all those cold gun blue compass needles pointing to you magnetic North—how cold can you take it? a problem which D.J. Goethe Rousseau James Clerk Max'ell pot n acid head all rolled into one Dallas T formation high school ass is going to prong into in the future or even right now—I mean do you have hard-on enough fraternity stud fucker Lambda Lambda Omicron Mu jockstrap frathouse faggot to put your red-hot daddy-loved-you ding into a cake of ice? Shit you do, Señor Shinola. Ice even numbs King Kong's dong. And all the needles point to the North where the icy Pole *is*—dig, node hunter? That tip which catches all the electromagnetic focus and funnel of that electromagnetic field called earth by the common clay (otherwise known as U.S. finger fuck voter) is exactly the place where the ice is, and that ice is the orifice, now you're cooking, cutey, that's to where the field runs, nay *flows* out from the center of the earth to go around the earth into the other end (South Pole, Newton!) and back through the fires, the molten red lava flaming shit furnace at the core where the heat is, changing all the way over to ice again as the electromagnetic field and stream passes from inside blazes to outside crust, and that deep cold on the crust node pole is the Encyclopedia of Cataclysmic Knowledge all refined down in the spooky early morning chill of Alaska August night up above the Circle, man, there're not ghosts up there, but communes of spookiness, pales, dominions, psycho swingers—even telepathies, Euripides, Alaska above the Circle is something else, and not just Aurora Borealis (which is also something else) —listen, dear limpidity of the intelligent ear which has cashed in its wax for hand-in-hand progression through these conceptual coils with D.J., we are going back to Aurora Borealis cause it is the only mountain of heavenly light which is certified to be result and product of magnetic disturbances—dig! you long patient asshole, we are on the track of something —that early morning chill is tuning the boys up because they getting the stone ice telepathic hollow from the bowels of the earth after it passed through the magnetic North Pole orifice. (Say now what's the dif between earth and flesh? Earth orifice is ice, whereas

159

flesh orifice? have you check out your bunghole fever reading lately? Think about that, all you concept-bound Yankee dry suck minds, y'need a little Texas oil in the pan, in the brainpan, Samantha.) That indeed is why Texas soil is so poor grit dry—all the goodness is down in that oil, all that fever and fuck lust percolating beneath. "Man," says Tex (after four hours' silence) "it was about time we did our split ass from that hunk shit safari." Tex, D.J. is here to tell you, has what they call a cold mien. Yeah, a real cold mean. He's a killer, baby, got one of those dull Texas faces to prove it. It's when he look interested and happy that you got to watch out, cause like the poet said, somebody is going to be dead. In fact, Tex is a looker, like D.J. He's tall, got a whippy old body, 6-1, 168 pound, all whip leather, saber and hide even when he seventeen. He and D.J. are lookalikes, except for expression, cause D.J. is full of mother-love received in full crazy bitch perfume aromas from Hallie, whereas Tex is full of ape shit daddy-love. Gottfried Hyde Senior, the fattest strongest fuck of an undertaker in Dallas ass County, had four girls in one marriage and then a fifth in the other (first wife died and he buried her with the services of his own mortician parlor—some undertakers got no shame) and second wife, the stringy Texas girl from fifty-two Texas shacks backs right to the Alamo got it up to give him a son on the second installment to emerge from her honest hardworking womb and snatch. She had a real pick and pull of a pussy, D.J.

always divined, just a mean skinny Texas snapper, a lobster claw of a cunt, just the type to turn on a fat bull of a Gottfried Hyde cause he looked to be one of those massive men with a little peeny dick, who, reason suggests, like a pussy which is quick, rubbery, pinchy as a thumb and finger—what else you going to get out of a short dick but a preference for girls who got the tunnel muscle at the front tip? This study of cunnubial arts by D.J. is grand hypothetical, cause D.J., owning God's blessing, is well hung, in fact he has a dick like a Nigger, but for hue, Renfrew, and it's one place he got it slightly over Tex—the Measure Your Dick Department. Anyhoo (cry if you got a short dick) Gottfried Hyde was torralee and cockaloo over his son Gott Hyde Junior, and raised him with the blessing of full love till he was five or six and developed a mind of his own, but no more of that unless we can take a visit to the back rooms at the embalmers, which, being our scene set only in Alaska and Dallas ass manse, we therefore cannot. But, full of daddy-love, Tex got that mean glint in the eye for which Texans are justly proud and famous, whereas D.J. has got the sweet smile of my-momma-loved-me-and-I'm-sweet-as-a-birthday-cake kind of mean look, you know like where the hell is it coming from next? As a team, by any reckoning, they're superbas, can't stop them, they a natural hunting couple. And now that it's morning, they stop, cook a little breakfast, figuring the smoke will be broken by the trees in the wood in which they cook so that Cop Turd won't spot

their fire. Besides it's too early. They'll assume at Ding
Bat the boys are off for a pre-breakfast hike. They do
not yet know that the boys is off on a bona fide tear.
Cause what they see is a range of mountains ahead with
real peaks, and they are going to go on up into them.
(Ice needle peaks are crystals to capture the messages
of the world.)

There! You all posed y'all ready for the next adventure in the heartland of the North, well hold your piss,
Sis, we're about to embark with Tex Hyde who is,
insist upon it, a most peculiar blendaroon of humanity
and evil, technological know-how, pure savagery, sweet
aching secret American youth, and sheer downright
meanness as well as genius instincts for occult power
(he's just the type to whip asses at the Black Masses) as
well as being crack athlete. Such consummate bundle
of high contradictions talks naturally in a flat mean ass
little voice. Better hear it.

Moreover, take a turn, pigeons, wheel on a bird
whistle, D.J. is calling you back to look at Gottfried
Hyde Senior and his second wife Jane McCabe Hyde,
mother of you know which Tex. Now Gottfried Senior, nickname Gotsie or Gutsy, is in his element when
up to the elbows in intestinal slime or a bull fuck. He's
bull fuck faggot fucker (pederast, you ass) bull fuck
sheep fucker, bull fuck waitress fucker, he'd even fuck
a keyhole if it was the size appropriate to a castle door.
(There's aisles and vales in that cold metallic chamber
lock.) Gutsy will fuck any orifice, nostril, ear, asshole,

mouth or any crevice, navel, even cream between two
fat tits (that's a 'tweener fuck) he'll rub your armpit
off, he'll split the crack in your athlete's foot, there's no
telling what legion of prongings and proctorings has
been delivered to the boxcar of corpses which pass
through the marble halls of Mortuary Manor. Now
D.J. ain't lost his sense of exquisite impeccable taste.
He's not bullshitting you one bit—Gutsy calls his
humming thriving corpse stuffer establishment nothing other than G. Hyde's Mortuary Manor, which of
course all the Dallasassians have promptly broken
down to Gutsy's Double M Kasket Klub. First question
to ask yourself is Gutsy such a champion prong sadist
bull fuck because he is an undertaker, or did he come
into being an undertaker because he is a prong fucker
first? Either way, chicken or egg, leave him loose with a
cow, a horse (preferably mare—not even Gutsy 5-11, 280
pounds of human living bull can stick it up a stallion's
ass) leave Gutsy with a jackass, a goat, a poor little
old dog, or a plump piece of human pudding too
appetizing to be called a corpse, for the Ghost has but
departed, give Gutsy a purchase on any hint of cave,
tunnel, scratch, or groove, and he will take his peeny
dick and lather up a storm. He even jacks off twice
a day. Winston Churchill used to drink a bottle
of brandy and smoke twenty cigars daily until he
was eighty more and dead. Gutsy Hyde jacks off
twice a night and will until he's ninety. But he's no
freaked-out onanist—that's just excess froth. Gutsy has

come an average of eight to ten times a day, seven days a week for forty plus years. The unknown statistic in the whole State of Texas, the secret spring to the coils and crazy fucked-up clockwork of Tex, D.J.'s ace, Tex Hyde, is simply that his daddy comes more often than anyone in the whole fucking state from cowpuncher to President and back again. And how does D.J. know all this? Well, everybody in Dallas who has ever come within hailing distance of Gutsy Hyde has felt the bull advancement of his persona. I mean, he grope you silly. You get caught in a corridor with G.H., Gott in Himmel, protect your parts, Gutsy will start to breathe heavy, he put his arm around you, he rub next to you, if you good and strong, and shove him off, or slippery-wise and slip away, he's come already, just that contact cloth to cloth, his pin in a crease of his pants, he's hot nuts, he's a Texas gusher. Gutsy comes all over the place out of a vast enthusiasm for life (or some such disease of unbalance as the fucked-out cynics would say) no, Gutsy presents a problem, what can make a man come so thumping much, and the answer is—D.J. whispers it—corpsemanship. Gutsy is tuned in to the Pharaoh's art, he's a libido hunter, a human dredge, dragging bottoms and pissing out bilge through that peeny dick of his, while consuming all aura and effluvia of libido. Gutsy is always catching and clutching a hair of the wetstone in his fat fuck greedy fingers or is equally gusto at burrowing away at the warmth, sweet, love, and fuck sugar of the universe inasmuch as these gifts of sunshine and generation are deployed, scattered, and distributed through men, women, dogs, goats, here we go again.

Now, Tex' ma, Jane McCabe Hyde, is on the side of being a saint. She cooks, cleans, mends, worries, does without a servant until pushed to the point of necessity, takes no time to herself, works for all, never grumbles, has the sunlight of the sea in the glint of her cornea, and in fact she'd qualify for Texas ass saint, female division, except for her pussy, that thumb and finger grip of real live snapper. Ever see a Southern Methodist halfback knife a line like a catapult had sprung him through, well, that's the Literary Handbook Metaphor Manual for old Jane McCabe Hyde and her secret pussy which keeps her from saint category. And how does D.J. know about this secret beautiful snap spring of pussy, well, Gottfried Hyde has told everyone in town about the wonders of his second wife's cunt, he has wanted people to know why he married her since she was then poor, unknown, plain of face, whereas Gutsy had married up first crack out, had got into some Country Club money shit, enough to set up his first Kasket Klub from which Mortal Man or Double M emerged. Yeah. So he didn't want on the death of his first wife (whom some would insinuate was fucked to death, although after bearing four girls, others could suggest that her maternal flappy-lip old rubber box was so big, Gottfried could have put his two meat-trust hands around his peeny dick in prayer and still got in) but dying from too much or too little off Gutsy's peeny old prick, Mr. Hyde the undertaker did not want, once his first rich beauty was gone, for people to think he was taking a single step down. So he bragged up a storm about the glories of Jane's Secret Sleeper until some were even curious to get in for themself, although offered no chance. Jane had the blessing of the Alamo in her. All that secret springiness been passed down in the seed, boy, anybody in the direct line of the heroes of the Alamo got seed like Mexican jumping beans, cause when all those Alamo troopers maintained to their positions and didn't piss in no pants and held their shit, tight honorable asshole in the face of certain death, and hung on, why a cloud and vale of love rose up about them in the middle of all this Mexican fire and shit storm, they was all loving their buddies so much, cause, man, they was the best bunch of sinewy high bounding zap and God streak fuckers, and each time one of them got one of Santa Ana's rounds in his virile little old Alamo heart, why, the fuck went up to death with a spring of joy, cause his buddies and his far-gone relatives (from whom the poor trooper hadn't had a letter in a year) were going to be nonetheless spiritual beneficiaries, and the spiritual essence of secret zinging semen went across the desert and through the air on the trooper's last breath and gave swinger pricks and springing cunts to some of the best and worst people in Texas. (Which accounts for why it's such a crazy state.) Yeah, go back to the martyrs of the Alamo, and add a picture of Tex and his parents, Gutsy and Jane, in cameo, and you get a notion of the kink which resides in the heart of the Lone Star. Now, carry on up to the mountains where soon . . . patience, patience, dear poontang, why it's on patience and poontang that they built the West. We can always get to the boys.

★

———————

INTRO BEEP 10

———————

★

Yeah, the boys is up in the boreal-montane conifer-ous forest biome (dig! shit ecologist big university librarian groper) and that biome may run from Labra-dor to western Alaska, but it about ready to give out, it's had it, all that three- to four-thousand-mile patch of balsam fir and black spruce, piss on that, wolverines, we ain't seeing much more of the tamarack on the stream sides, and the willows, the birch, the alder and the poplars (all concealing their Doppler effect, Wolf-gang!) no, the boys are stepping up the south slopes

of the foothills of the Brooks Range and those mountains ahead, forget it, that's where the real church of
the spirits goes congregating in cathedrals of black ice,
blue ice, white snow, land of the dream spirits, listen
asshole America, D.J. your disc jockey is telling you,
where you going when you sleep? well, hole, there's
only one place you go, and that's into the undiscovered
magnetic-electro fief of the dream, which is opposed to
the electromagnetic field of the earth just as properly
as the square root of minus one is opposed to one.
Right! They never figured out yet whether light is
wave, corpuscle, or hung up on finding her own identity, all they know once you get down to it is that light
is bright, and therefore not necessarily opposed to being part of Universal Mind, henceforth known as UM
which is the fat frog you calling for, Volta, when you
clear your throat (um) and look for inspiration (um).
Cough up an oyster, roll that phlegm, diddle it around
your finger, Clem—you can't get fucked for less—here
is the sweet intimate underground poop: when you go
into sleep, that mind of yours leaps, stirs, and sifts itself
into the Magnetic-Electro fief of the dream, hereafter
known as M.E. or M.E.F., you are a part of the spook
flux of the night like an iron filing in the E.M. field
(otherwise glommed as e.m.f.) and it all flows, mind
and asshole, anode and cathode, you sending messages
and receiving all through the night, if you had your
nose in garlic and been bum fucking the wrong cunt,
well the route this yere night is through the dreams of

"Corporate Hopital Corporation

the witches, that's a circuit, Perkins, lots of shit, and if
you clean as milk and had your nose all day up the antiseptic asshole of Big H the Corporate Hospital Corporation, why then your dreams got to go through the
incinerator where they pile all the old hospital ban-
dages, all that dried blood pus shit green gangrene
bladder gut mess—that's a battery—from all the surgery
of the day which surgery had duly excised and thereby
assassinated one hundred plus organs from seventy-
eight patients, a confusion in the Divine Economy, as
all those organs taking millions of years to make (think
of the evolution of the cells) are now being flushed in
a gush into the incinerator while the surgeons get their
clean whiskey-free libidinal juice—I mean, man, just
think of being able to knife somebody and get paid for
it—anyhow, Mr. Clean Milk, with your nose up Corporation's antiseptic asshole, it seems by this itinerary that
your dreamland route, your M.E.F. trip ticket, your
private sleep circuit goes right through that incinerator
bag in the hospital gut pile, dream on that, all your
messages all going through those amputated organs,
ugh, all the Bunnies dreaming of nunneries, no matter
what route, if the message go from you across the bed
to your dear mate (rot in your own bad breath, spoiler
mine) or if you flinging a thought all the way from
Dallas to Alaska and back again, just no chance, know
this, you a part of the dream field, you the square root
of minus one, you off in a flux, part of a circuit, you
swinging on the inside of the deep mystery which is

171

whatever is electricity, and who is magnetism? for they the in and out, the potential and actual, the about to be and the becoming of Something—we cannot call it love, the lust of Satan, can that be? Magnetism potential and electricity the actual of the Prince himself? whoo-ee, say D.J., cause his genius brain can grope ultimates and that's not for every short-hair butterball in town, no, figure this, the electricity and magnetism of the dream fief is reversed—God or the Devil takes over in sleep—what simpler explanation you got, M.A. expert type? nothing better to do than put down Mani the Manichee, well, shit on that, D.J. is here to resurrect him through a point of declaration in the M.E. fief which is this—all the messages of North America go up to the Brooks Range. That land above the Circle, man, is the land of the icy wilderness and the lost peaks and the unseen deeps and the spires, crystal receiver of the continent. Wait and hear. Goose your frequency.

★

CHAP TEN

★

Listen, did you know, creep technician, about the superconductivity of metals at absolutely low temperatures? yeah, fab, you get down at three degrees or four degrees of absolute zero (and that's *the* zero, man—lower you cannot go) guess what—there is five metals, no more, which become super superconductors. Take a ring of Thallium, that soft shit, put it at 240° abs. for absolute, run a bar magnet through the middle of the ring, run it out again, and the current that's induced won't stop running around the ring for months. So, employ your new knowledge, take a cunt, put her near Absolute Zero, work up a ring of troth (this is a wedding, you nut) composed of Old Thallium, Mother Mercury, Lemuel Lead, Timothy Tin, or Ike Indium, any one of those soft spooky witch metal elements will do, cool it till it's as cold as that beauteous cunt out near Absolute Zero, and then, man, hold your hairy jewels, cause a shock is coming up, why you just take and run and plunge your dick through the near absolute zero ring, zing into that gone ice snatch, whoo-ee! whoo-ee! pull it out before you rock stone ice pinnacle prick. You just set up a current, man, is going to keep that cunt in charge for months. Whoever said your gong was not a magnet? Oo la la, Françoise, your trou de merde is inoubliable for it is like the Camembert my mozzaire used to make when we were young, Boonkie.

Fuck this noise, why is D.J. hovering on the edge of a stall? Make your point! But D.J. is hung because the events now to be recounted in his private tape being made for the private ear of the Lord (such is the hypothesis now forging ahead) are hung up on a moment of the profoundest personal disclosure, in fact, dig, little punsters out in fun land, D.J. cannot go on because he has to talk about what Tex and him were presented with there all alone up above the Arctic Circle, and that's where the root of the hangnail grows, it all happens faster in the Arctic C, there's gathering of ionization on those polar caps, those auroral regions

are electric, man, more ground charge than the rest of
earth, cause the messages are coming in, the M.E.F.
(Magnetic-Electro Fief—don't forget) is charging the
joint by night, those ice ass pinnacles of the Brooks
Range are vibrating to the modulations of the waves, a
crystal oscillator is every mountain has got ice on its
tip, and there's lots of mountains and lots of ice, pick
up on this—the boys, you will remember, dear grassed-
out auditor, have just finished cooking their breakfast,
and aware of game all about them, half-clean themselves from the walk, half-fouled with the emanated
nauseas of medium assholes and Rusty high-grade asshole, disillusioned with Big Luke's Cop Turd copping
out on the big game hunter's code and oath, and just in
a general state of mixed shit, for the walk up to here
has done them only a minim of good. They have not
cleaned the pipes, not yet. They are still full of toilet
plunger holes seen in caribou, and shattered guts and
strewn-out souls of slaughtered game meats all over the
Alaska air and Tex feels like he's never going to hunt
again which is not unhorrendous for him since he's
natural hunter, but then with one lightning leap from
the button on his genius belt to the base of his brainpan he gets the purification ceremony straight in his
head, and announces to D.J. that they gonna wrap
their weapons and lash them in a tree, and then they
going to walk through the forest and up to the peak
with their Randall bowies, and their binocs, and packs,
but nothing to protect themselves with except the

knife. They each know even as he says it that this is how you get the fear, shit, disgust and mixed shit tapeworm out of fucked-up guts and overcharged nerves. But D.J. is in a grab for your dick competition snit that he didn't think of this first, so says, "Let's leave the Randalls behind, too."

And Tex replies, "A man can't go without a knife."

"Do it or don't do it," says D.J., "but don't finger fuck yore ass."

Man, this is striptease shit. "Then we don't take our binocs," says Tex.

"Then don't take our packs."

No sleeping bags.

No food.

No compass.

Man, they got some of that mixed shit out of them already. About the time they cache all belongings, they own clean fear now, cause they going to live off the land. And they as light as if they lost gravity. D.J. could take a ten-foot spring. If it wasn't cold ass this morning, he'd be ready to go naked. Oh, that country looks big and mean up ahead.

But they got to take a backward step. Cause their ass is freezing half to death. You ever count on the weather in Brooks Range, kiss your own fever blister, mister (you know how you got it) that weather is like a bitch with hot and cold water running in her bush. Right now it's running icy shock cold. They push up not two hundred yards after we left them caching their

gear, going through the boreal-montane, not two hundred yards through a forest getting skinny in its Arctic
birch and alder, hardly a black spruce left, and squat,
they at the edge, they at timberline again, and the
ridge of the hill they been climbing is there, bare,
twenty yards ahead of them, and they top that, and
look down on a long valley, more forest, and then
ahead to the beginning of a range of snow-topped
mountains, bare-ass peaks, bare as the bald head of an
egg, bare and white as the crest on a wave, and more
mountains behind them, and more behind, like an
arrow across the morning blue shooting for two hundred miles or more across mountains no man ever saw
from the center, only from the air, and nothing but
snow, even now in September nothing but snow, land
as white as a desert and deserted, just peaks. And it
rings back at them like a stone on a shield, no, better
block that metaphor, drop it altogether, Lady Ethel, it
rings back like a finger wet on the rim of the best piece
of glass on Park Avenue, New York, yeah—D.J. ain't
been East for nothing—those mountains are a recep-
tacle, man, a parabolic reflector, an avatar, a bowl of
resonance, listen to the boys totter just at the icy look
of them, and they know they got to go back a little on
their newfound principles, they got to take a bedroll
and grub, their pup tent, the matches, a rope, shit, they
can't go clean, they even take the binoculars, but
mixed shit does not flow in again to the reservoir of
their heart because celestial mechanics is built on

WHY ARE WE IN VIETNAM?

equations and going with nothing into the forest is not necessarily more loaded with points of valor than going with rudimentary bag and forage yet without arms into mountain snow. September, and that land ahead is white as a sheet! So they still clean, and lost thirty minutes pulling down lashed gear from the tree and lashing it up again to keep grizzer from cleaning them out before they return, but now they really off, they up over the ridge, down into the forest draw, and climb up again, and one hour and twenty minutes later they are on the edge of the snow, that same snow which looked to be near as an arrow shot away. But now the sun is out, and it is hot, man, up to 65° and more which is hot in that snow and the dazzle is like sunlight on the water.

"That dazzle," said D.J., pushing into the sluggish kind of mealy new wet powder, not fluff, not sludge, just a bit of going heavy, three inches deep here, no more, here at the beginning of a snowfield, one thousand miles wide (or near to that) and two hundred miles north across the mountains onto tundra again, "that dazzle," said D.J., "is like sunlight on water."

"Shit," said Tex.

"Yeah, man, it's like the dazzle on the water outside of Herod's court in Caesarea, ever hear of that?"

"Shee-it," said Tex.

"Well, you ain't no I.Q. competitor."

"Fuck, I ain't. I compete you in anything."

"Never mess with me, ignoramus."

CHAP TEN

"Why," said Tex, "tell me about Herod and his fuck hole in Caesarea. When you done I'm gone to do a Caesarea up your ass."

"You ain't seen the day you was strong enough to unzip it out of your pants around me, pussy kisser."

"Pick the dingleberries out of your teeth. Who was Herod?"

"Herod was a royal goat fucker, you cock-sucker."

"I," said Tex, "never sucked a cock in my life, but I'm going to make you the first. I'm going to suck your cock and bite it off and send the bloody abomination to your momma."

"Oh, man, you'd be a cha-cha faggot if you wasn't so ugly."

Hey, hey, is this the way they really talk? And at sixteen and seventeen. Well, yes, they is geniuses, D.J. been telling you. And all that pederastic palaver? Hell, yes. They is crazy about each other. They even prong each other's girls when they can, but fear not, gentle auditor, they is men, real Texas men, they don't ding ding ring a ling on no queer street with each other, shit, no, they just talk to each other that way to express Texas tenderness than which there is nothing more tender than a flattened pan-fried breaded paper-thin hard-ass Texas steak. And don't forget those French fries and the dead fly in the red crud rim of the bottle ketchup, not to mention the citric acid in the salad dressing—we ain't got those gut bucket skillet flat Texas ass stomachs for nothing. Listen, fellow Ameri-

cans, and D.J. here to tell you, don't get upset by the
boys' last dialogue, they so full of love and adventure
and in such a haste to get all the mixed glut and sludge
out of their systems that they're heating up all the foul
talk to get rid of it in a hurry like bad air going up the
flue and so be ready to enjoy good air and nature,
cause don't forget they up in God's attic, that country
way upstairs, Brooks Range here, to say not too far
from Mount Michelson, that's a mount, and so fret not
those of ye who live for the quiet of Sunday on our
quiet streets, those boys would not talk that way to
your daughter or your sister, no, sir, they would just
ruminate privately a little, and do their best to fuck
her.

Yeah, and now they don't talk for half an hour, and
just walk along climbing in the barest parts of the snow
which is three inches and two and not too bad, but for
the drifts where it is foot and more, and then Tex, all
quiet and cool, puts a light grip of a hand on D.J., and
whispers, "Shut up, now, there's a wolf on the ridge."

And that wolf is a sight. He's a white wolf and he
weigh in at one hundred and plus and plus, just a long
big high beast of a white police dog the size of a
Dalmatian and more. And that wolf is doing nothing,
he's just running along the ridge, and taking a bound
now and then and his big white fur goes up in the air
and separates just as lithe and quick ass from the snow.
There's times you can see nothing more than a mouth,
nose and eyes, black outline black as paint, two ovals,

180

two green-gold eyes, black stub of a nose, air so clear
you can see the shine in the cavity of the black nostrils,
and then the mouth, black outline, red gums, red as
cut-open flesh, and white teeth, fangs. They suddenly
aware they got no gun, and this wolf not much beyond
one hundred yards away on the ridge is alert to something, could it be them? and they raise hackles and try
to hold them down, cause those hackles are transmit-
ting waves, and oh, shit, that wolf just turned, he's
putting his radar on their waves, whoo, he's zero on
them, can't see, but can sense, he takes one step their
direction like feeling the pulsing up of the field—what
they giving off, murder or a meal? He can't determine,
so here comes another step. Animal murder is near.
Everything is all silent suddenly. Nature is just as
timid shit as a slum street—the boys did not know
before how silent silence could be, thought it was silent
in the snow, but there had been sparrows, yeah,
scutterings of squirrels, yeah, white snow mice, sounds
all over, now none. Each of those boys rings up the
voltage in their resolve, like let that fuck wolf try to
come to them, and they will give him a time, they
thinking of how to kick his nuts in, choke his throat,
dig into his ears with their fingers, push through his
eyes to his brain (that is if he is biting one and the
other does the rescue) man, they're fired, and that
electric fire goes off them. Two waves of murder, human and animal, meet across the snow in a charge as
fantastic and beautiful as Alexander Nevsky, thank

"movies"

you very much, and wolf stops dead, knocked on his
psychic ass, what a pity psychic struggle cut no ice with
silver iodide or movies be cheaper to make: that wolf
slides off them and goes ambling down the ridge, no
longer leaping and swinging at how loose, hippy-dippy,
juggler balls and ass he is, no, the wolf he older, he
been put down, that's no good for any presumptive
continuer of his own species.

But the D.J. wave and the Tex Hyde wave which
Lupo II decided to slide away from has gone wave
zinging into the air where Mr. Lobster with wings,
Thing with a claw, E Pluribus, old man Eagle fuck,
yeah old man Eagle comes a zooming down out of the
air in plummet, gray feather mass, white neck, black
head, black claws, black as teakwood, man, whoo-ee,
what a drop, the boys they practically clapping, he
comes from five hundred feet right down like Magnum
Lightning Zero down to the back of Lupo II who turns
just in time, opens those teeth, wheels, stands on hind
feet, swings two forelegs, left right, cuff, cuff, and M
Lightning Zero, our eagle, hereafter MLZ, thank you,
splats into a flat out, wings out, hovers, like an *eagle,*
man, wings arched and fluttering just a tickle to stay in
place above the wolf, he just gliding in the air one spot,
his claws like lightning, zap! zap!—they miss each
other, wolf and eagle, but that opening of the wings to
brake out from the plummet when Lupo II took his
wheel, turn, and fight, oh man, it was a shock to the
heart, cause death stood out in those wings, if you'd

c.f.
p. 182

been a bug in the shadow of those wings you'da called out, "Bury me clean, Armageddon is here." And D.J. thinks just once of his dad, and eagle story he told him and knows MLZero is going for the eyes, and wolf he's just going for the meal, and in comes MLZ and L II stands him off, miss and miss, and again they try, wolf giving a sobbing scream like, "I'm going to kill you, mother-fucker." And old Magnum LZ he got a screech like a den of hooknosed women when one of their pocketbooks is missing, so it's sob and scream, and attack and parry, come in on a shot, brake, claw air, veer off, do a spin back, and Mr. Wolf like a boxer picking off horseflies in the air, cuff, cuff, coot, coot, suddenly it's bullshit and bullshit, cause they each missing the other, old eagle he staying just out of range, Magnum Z. Lightning that's all the fuck he is, Tuckerman, and finally they done, and M.Z. Lightning humps his wings and heads on down the air carrying on like a crow, and L II nominating himself as winner, sets on his hind end and lets up a call which starts low, calls in all the beasty guts for miles around, tells them of the taste of fresh game, goes up higher than a coloratura into ascents of panic and power and warning and a call to the mountain ring and then tries to hit High E above High C for nothing, to show he's a virtuoso, and fails to make it, good for him, and slides all down into bronchitis again and the smell of his own shit ass wolf hide in a hole in hibernation not so far away. And the boys understood every sound of it. And if Tex had had a gun, he would have imitated every sound of it. But they don't have a gun and once again they feel just as clean and on-edge and perfect as would you, sedentary send-in-terror auditor of this trip, when you, sir, are about to insert the best piece of cock you ever mustered up into a cunt which is all fuck for you, and your nose is ozone you so clean and perfect, well, they feeling like that every instant now, whoo-ee! whoo-ee; they can hardly hold it in, cause this mother nature is as big and dangerous and mysterious as a beautiful castrating cunt when she's on the edge between murder and love, forgive the lecture, Pericles, but the smell is everywhere, the boys are moving on smell, snow smell, better believe it, good here, not so good there—move along, this is sweet, hold up, rotten shit around the bend, some clutch of mice, no more, but their scamperings set up the wrong scratchy little tickler cymbal along the snow fluff and make some smell go wrong somewhere else, something like that. Man, it's terrifying to be free of mixed shit. And they got the unfucked heaven of seeing twelve Dall ram on an outcropping of snow two miles away across two ridges, and those Dall ram solemn head and light foot make their way down a slope, heading into valleys for winter and for feed, it's a procession, and through the binocs they are so white and their horns, oh, man, the underside is yellow golden rosy color that gives D.J. twiddles in the gut (twiddles being of course nothing but mother-of-pearl butterflies in cameo, Sir Lancelot) *helicopter*

and the sun is on that snow and space! man. You could
be Cleopatra on a barge and twenty galley slaves, and
the sun on the water is a feather in your nose. Olé, olé.
Then they hear the helicopter. Man conceived of
fucking in order to get fucked. There is no doubt of
that. So, off they plunge, trying always to keep a ridge
between them and the copter, and looking for streams
so they leave no track, and know already they've left a
track. Well, for the next two hours right into two in
the afternoon, it's no action, just pain, they going in
deeper into Brooks Range and Cop Turd buzzing
about, looking here, looking there, but never too far
away. And then around two P.M. he departs, figuring,
they hope, that Cop Turd finally decided the hints of
trail they left might be animal. No, that ain't it, Cop
Turd must have set down long enough to examine
their steps—hell, CT is out of gas, Al Bell with his Bell
47 J is out of gas. That all—he'll be back.

Then they discover a valley. It's for the boys, better
believe it. A bowl below snow level, maybe two miles
by one mile, meadows and wood, tundra and rock, and
clearings and shapings, could be the Colorado Rockies
it's so sweet right in the middle of the beginning of all
that snow wilderness, tucked between ridges of snow,
and so the boys work a trail in a false direction into a
creek, back up on their steps a mile (you try walking
backward a mile) and slip into the forested bowl leaving behind the fields of snowfields and see for a last
sight one pale pink fox go springing through the snow

to pin a field mouse in snow and Arctic grass, flip, flop, oops and out, nub, nudge, you're dead mouse and a little echo out in the air, one small sorrow. And then some squirrels dart from the wood, run out by the fox, coax him to chase, and go back up a stand of black spruce at the edge of the bowl, black spruce again after the boys thought the biome was dead and finished. And a wing of sparrows go rip-titting and coo-cawing after Fox cause he can't catch Squirrel, and Fox he humps and scratches and whines and cries, he cries, dig, cause Squirrel won't come down to get killed. Maybe he's thinking of the children at home on a starve.

Man, our two little hunt boys, Killer I and Killer II, are excruciated. They near to being sick from the sweet they want to laugh so hard at Mr. Egomaniac Fox—come on down, Squirrel, be a good fellow. Yeah, they feel so good they stop for an inst, head to head, toe to toe, and mill it up, each taking ten good lumps to the gut.

"Hurt?" screams Tex.

"No, sir."

"Why not?"

"Cause I'm a Royal Commando, sir." And they cackle. But the moment they stop (1) the King of Mountain Peak M.E.F. shit, (2) Mr. Awe and (3) Mr. Dread—that troika—that Cannibal Emperor of Nature's Psyche (this is D.J. being pontiferous, for we are contemplating emotion recollected in tranquillity back at the Dallas ass manse, RTPY—Remembrance

Things Past, Yeah, you remember?) yeah the CE of NP, Cannibal Emperor for sure, Mr. Sender, who sends out that Awe and Dread is up on their back clawing away like a cat because they *alone,* man, you dig? why, they just dug, they all *alone,* it's a fright wig, man, that *Upper* silence alone is enough to bugger you, whoo-ee, all the twiddles have turned to plummets and they don't even know from what, and then know, it's their laughing up in the silence. They turning everything on in the wrong way, and they ready to retreat. And mixed shit is ready to drop in again on the lip of their liver.

But that meadow is beautiful. Arctic flowers, more white mountain aven with yellow centers, and the tundra gone to red and yellow and berries, dwarf huckleberries, cranberries, which they eating to calm Mr. A and Mr. D and the Cannibal, Mr. Sender, and the tart comes up out of the berry, one fine vein of sugar drawn from sour ice. And earth, taste of sunlight the sentimental might declare, but the troika is on them again, Cannibal Emperor to the fore, whoa whoa what I dread, they can but hardly breathe, and D.J. first to dig into the dimensions of the message which is simple, yes, direct—bear is nearby. That is it—a bear is near. And Tex don't argue—all in a funk without a gun, they pick a tree, they up it fifteen feet, high as they can go, they wait there on the edge of the meadow, the minutes go by. And then they remember they have left the packs behind and down they go all

shaking, up the tree they work again, getting the packs
up, and before they once more in the upper whippy
weak crack snap branches of the black spruce like pegs,
not much better to sit on, well, lo, behold, bear, there
bear, out at other edge of the meadow and he don't see
them, no, nor smell upwind from them, they ready to
swear they smell him.

Now, bit by bit, they cool, get back cock. Because
they safe, yeah, man, safe unless the branch break, and
Mr. Bear he's all right, because their mind-ass trans-
mitter after Awe-Dread Bombardment from Mr.
Sender is chucked down to relaxed little beeps (the
boys is quietened now from being up in the Brooks
Range all alone—you in need of a great cool-out—you
try it) and because the boys are relaxed, half in soft
fear, half sweet fatigue—ain't slept, remember? they
just now look, and what do you think Grizzer is doing?

Well, he after a meal, man, and he like every fat ass
in the world: when he eating, you could ring a fire
siren under his nuts and he never miss a beat in the
gourmandize, he's humping up on all the berries—
they ain't been too many this season, remember?—and
so he grab with a paw and hooks in about two hundred
buffalo berries at a pop, and swallows, and lets blue
juice and red juice run out of the sides of his black wet
leather mouth, and then raises one paw in the air and
wipes said mouth on his shoulder as if he imitating a
weight lifter sniffing his own armpit, then griz burps,
yeah, old bear burps and spits out the next mouth of

berries, and then he sighs (and they chilling him with
their pistol eyes, so young and up tight with trying not
to breathe they could be airline hostesses serving Frank
Sinatra African rock-tail frozen ass lobster) yeah, and
fighting silently over who holds the binocs, and daring
each other to climb down the tree and watch from the
ground, and then each of them being not up to the
dare, and not certain—does private honor of Texas
good heart and clean shit require they touch boot
leather to ground?—but while they debating in the
lowest whisper ever heard, "You go," no "Fuck, you
go," it gets too fascinating and they just watch some
more, because Old Bear has the burps, and now he out
in the tundra with his dark mahogany hide digging up
sod and scrubbing at roots, and he works at that like a
gardener, digging in one of his big mitts, bigger in plan
than a volume of *Encyclopaedia Britannica*, Dallas
edition (which is bigger than the standard edition,
natch) he's all claws in that sod and turf of poor old
skinny misery tundra, he like a rake, yeah, he just cuts
out pieces of turf and turns them over. The under-
neath is tundra root of all variety, thick as nerves and
shoots, thick as lamp wire, thick as your finger, and
Grizzer just eats away at this mat looking just like a
roast beef hash, crust, black and almost charred, digging into the mat of the earth and contemplating what
the dirt and the nerve roots and the accumulated
experience of the various bugborers and slugs have to
say. And in the middle of this, sitting sad and munch-

ing slow after slowly uprooting, expunging, and devouring five square yards of peat with many a heavy sigh and one or two fine from the heart burps, Griz suddenly decides his ass is on an itch and he looks to scratch it, and flings away his mat, and works his butt on the tundra, scraping and scratching and rolling on his back, and thumping and bumping his ass, and then he gets up like a fat woman and walks off in a grump to the other end of the meadow and sidles to a young tree and takes a bite out of the bark on the trunk about seven feet up, just rising on his hind legs sort of lazy and taking a deep easy bite, mean and pleasurable, like a businessman copping a goose on a bare-ass nightclub waitress, yum! and then he turn around, old Griz, and shove his insatiable ass against the bark of the tree, and he rub and he slide and he shimmy like you rubbing a Turkish towel up the crack of your own sweet potato, and then he grunt and lie down and go to sleep right there.

And boys wait, ten minute, twenty minute, the squirrels flitting, mice heads popping in the tundra, sparrow settling on the back of Grizzer, indeed! and a hint of the wind spring up in the afternoon and see a white hare, hop, hump, hop, he gone, looking like white Benny bump tail on a caribou, and a marmot in a burrow, and a weasel so Tex would swear, D.J. do not see it. Then they decide to go down and keep working downwind from sleeping Grizzer, but griz starts to stir. And over the ridge which they can just see

through the binocs, up in snow country again out of
the bowl, is a sight they hear first and cannot believe
cause a hundred or more, maybe many more, caribou
are passing on the ridge and that convention of antlers
looks just so fine and unbelievable as a forest on a
march. And while the boys watch they hip into a little
aggregate of fact which is those antlers (known in
plural as a calliope of antlers) are a-zigging and a-
jogging and a-twigging because there are lines of dance
shaping and reshaping around three or four caribou
gentlemen known as Bull Fuck 1, Bull Fuck 2, etc.,
each of them with cows and kids, but there's a vigorish
in the air, a rumble to be heard among these beasts,
they stepping and hopping like rutting season is near,
and two of them BF 1 and BF 3 stop for a second in the
brisk September afternoon air and hunker down their
hind legs, and then give each other a clout with their
antlers like football linemen making contact, slap,
snap, sharp and fast, then they break off like they've
had a taste of goodies to come but must go back to
march route, and all this, especially the clear crack of
antler clatter, sharp as shoulder guards hitting each
other in loud clear hill ringing echo has done one bit
of work, Grizzer he's up, he shakes, he wheels in a circle
once, twice, then he off like a bull locomotive driving
up to the ridge, and busts up and out of the bowl and
makes a mad-ass charge at the procession of caribou,
and they who have been traveling in the deep of their
noncarnivorous communion to new forage, new land,

new love, and winter quarters, are off now on a tear, as are the boys, now down from the tree and scrambling up the ridge to have a look at the sight of hundreds plus of beast all running silently through the snow and Grizzer after them cutting through the middle of that calliope of antlers scattering like fish, then regrouping out and around Mr. Bear and taking off and they all getting away, of course, of course, except for one calf who stumble in fright and griz right down on young beast and with one paw at the neck and the other on the flank, goes in with mouth open to rip her belly and get the living blood and taste of live entrail, whatever that may be, whatever taste to have fat-ass Grizzer so avid ass for it, and when calf breaks loose half for an instant, pain springing it near to free, why, Grizzer flips her down again and having had his taste of her live, kills her now by slamming his teeth through the big muscles of her back right through to the spine and vertebrae which he crunches in two closing his big mouth and she breaks like a stick of wood and is there lifeless and her death goes out over the ridge and slips into the bowl and the afternoon takes a turn and is different having just passed through one of those unseen locks of the day, everything is altered, not saying how.

And Grizzer he eats awhile, and paws at flesh, he feeling fat and sort of food disgusted, and then works a little half-ass at covering the carcass over, but he's not heart in it, and after a while just contents himself by taking a piss at the head, and a big bear drop of baubles at the tail, Griz like a baron hasn't learned to read or write but sure knows sealing wax, let me put my humper monicker mooney on this. And goes off, Griz #2 about as different from Griz #1 with the big eye dying that D.J. would kiss LBJ on the petoons just to have a rifle to take down Griz 2 and see how he look when he die, similar or very different as if the center of all significant knowledge right there.

The bear is gone, and they down from the tree and exploring the bowl, but modestly, stepping in the big cool, feeling clean but weak, and too sweet, sweet as caribou. Instinct take them up the bowl and onto snow ridge and there is a caribou, mother of the dead calf, and she hardly look up when she see them, she just stand with her head down and her nose on the flesh of her dead, pushing off the snow and bits of dirt Griz 2 left, and her hooves in passing and by accident go through the bear bauble old Baron Bear has left and kicks her into a fright as if hate was suddenly stinging her feet, and she circles about in a dance, but never takes her nose off as if she is going to smell on through to the secret of flesh, as if something in the odor of her young dead was there in the scent of the conception not ten months ago when some bull stud caribou in moonlight or sun illumined the other end of the flesh somewhere between timber slide and lightning there on the snow, some mystery then recovered now, and woe by that mother caribou nuzzled in sorrow from

193

her nose while the sky above blue as a colorless sea
went on and sun burned on her, flies came, last of the
flies traveling over the snow and now running a shuttle
from Baron Bear's pile of bauble to the nappy spotty
hide of caribou mother, she twitching and jumping
from the sure spite of the sting but not relinquishing
her nose and the dying odor of her yearling calf and
D.J.'s head full spun with that for new percipience,
since could it be odor died last of all when one was
dead? and took a separate route, and where could that
lead his mind, for the secret of D.J.'s genius is that he
pure American entrepreneur, and so his mind will
always follow a lead. Never been a businessman yet
wasn't laughed at in the beginning, you bet. And here
was the lead about the death of odor but then, just
then, a flight of cranes went over, one hundred, two
hundred, so now there were hundreds and hundreds,
yes, men, they could no longer count numbers flying
overhead in formations of V and diamond and echelon
and hovering on course, two hundred like one, and
birds wrapped up in the mission to go south carrying
some part of the sky in their thousand wings as if the
very beginning of autumn, seed of the fall, for North
America below in all the weeks to come was in the high
cawing and wing beat clear up to the fanning and
vibrating of reeds some high long-gone sound such as
summer coming to the very end.

That was all they saw that day. They traveled over
ridges, slid down new snow on slopes and went in

further. A still was on them. The cranes had emptied
the pocket of this territory and they moved on seeing
not a tree nor an animal nor a sight but for the glaciers
ahead and the loud crack of their boom in the late
afternoon, and the ridgelines, the ridgelines now beginning to dance in the late afternoon with transpar-
encies behind turns of transparency and sunlight rising
up straight from the snow in lines of razzle reflection,
their eyes gritted, and afternoon chill was still good on
them yes, and yes, for the colors began to go from snow
gold and yellow to rose and blue, coral in the folds of
the ridges when the sun still hit, coral bright as the
underside of the horn of the Dall ram and there were
two, a couple, high again on the farthest ridge, first
animal they'd seen in hours and then they saw one
more. It was after they put up a tent. They came to one
more bowl with a few trees, a hint of bare ground, and
a crazy salty pond, mud and salt at its edges but very
sure of itself in the snow hills like all that Northern
land so ready to declare it has a purpose when none to
be seen, and they put up a lean-to in grove of black
spruce, last black spruce this side of the Pole, D.J.
ready to swear, and lit a fire and cooked grub, roast
beef hash, yeah, beans, bread, coffee, chocolate bar, so
tired they jawed the food like cattle plodding, and lay
down side by side drawing heat from the fire up the
blankets into their legs, boots tied to a stay overhead,
heat of the fire putting iron back into their body like
the iron and fire of faith for those black spruce twigs

and short branches and rotten punk for start (which punk D.J. had not forgot was from the lore of his father of whom he could not yet think) fuel for the fire out of the soil of this land up on the top, cold bare electric land of North, magnetic-electro fief of the dream, and D.J. full of iron and fire and faith was nonetheless afraid of sleep, afraid of wolves, full of beauty, afraid of sleep, full of beauty, yeah, he un-ashamed, for across the fire and to their side the sun was setting to the west of the pond as they looked north, setting late in the evening in remembering echo of the endless summer evening in these woods in June when darkness never came for the light never left, but it was going now, September light not fading, no, ebbing, it went in steps and starts, like going down a stair from the light to the dark, sun golden red in its purple and purple red in the black of the trees, the water was dark green and gold, a sigh came out of the night as it came on, and D.J. could have wept for a secret was near, some mystery in the secret of things— why does the odor die last and by another route?—and he knew then the meaning of trees and forest all in dominion to one another and messages across the conti-nent on the wave of their branches up to the sorrow of the North, the great sorrow up here brought by leaves and wind some speechless electric gathering of woe, no peace in the North, not on the top of the rim, and as the dark came down, a bull moose, that King Moose with antlers near to eight feet wide across all glory of spades and points, last moose of the North, came with his dewlap and his knobby knees and dumb red little eyes across the snow to lick at salt on the other side of the pond, and sunlight in the blood of its drying caught him, lit him, left him gilded red on one side as he chomped at mud and salt, clodding and wads dumping from his mouth to plop back in water, like a camel foraging in a trough, deep in content, the full new moon now up before the sun was final and down silvering the other side of this King Moose up to the moon silhouettes of platinum on his antlers and hide. And the water was black, and moose dug from it and ate, and ate some more until the sun was gone and only the moon for light and the fire of the boys and he looked up and studied the fire some several hundred of feet away and gave a deep caw pulling in by some resonance of this grunt a herd of memories of animals at work and on the march and something gruff in the sharp wounded heart of things bleeding somewhere in the night, a sound somewhere in that voice in the North which spoke beneath all else to Ranald Jethroe Jellicoe Jethroe and his friend Gottfried (Son of Gutsy) "Texas" Hyde. They were alone like that with the moose still staring at them. And then the moose turned and crossed the bowl the other way and plodded through the moonlight along the ridges of snow, moonlight in his antlers, gloom on his steps. And the boys slept.

★

_____

CHAP ELEVEN

_____

★

And woke up in three hours. And it was black, and the fire near to out. They were cold. Cold, you see, with age in their bones, and Tex, shivering, dug himself out of the chill deep folds of the blanket and D.J.'s body hugging ice to ice against him. Like a thin bitter old woman, cursing ice and old age and his lazy partner and the rheumatism of future joints, Tex poked in the dark and worked the pile of other black spruce twigs and branches into the fire, his nostrils going near to drunk from the sensitivity of mucus deep in sleep being lit up by the aroma of unsuspecting pure burning resin, turpentine converging for an instant to something like opium, you bet, the planes of flame thin, not yet hot, hardly warm till he built a cage of twigs and beat the log as if he scourging indolence to cut to the live coal and reworked and remade his fire structure, tuning it, and stood before the new flame getting some of that ingredient of Alaska earth which worked once to make a tree and give it fuel to burn for his heat, so Tex stood there pulling heat from the earth, and to the side D.J. saw a wolf go easing off and sat up in bed in ice fear and reached for a pot and clanged it.

They cursed each other for a while, Tex him for staying under the blankets, he Tex for being so dumb as never to see a wolf so near, and then D.J. got up and stood by the fire, and when they both warm, they lay down again, and got calm, and felt warm and the trouble started, trouble of the simplest sort it was that profound—they could not sleep. Lying there in wilderness, for all they knew no other man for fifteen or twenty miles, the moon was on the pond, little sounds coming from that pond, fish of the North breaking surface time to time could that be, and on the ground the restlessness of lemmings and voles, and foxes no doubt and the wolf, nothing sleeping easy in this bowl around this pond. Fire, that pit of possibilities beyond the imagination of quadruped animals, yes, the inner throat of the active lion easier to contemplate for such as beasts, and the silence was not a still but came in

CHAP ELEVEN

flows and swells like the ripples of a pool, yeah, and
each sound left clouds of silence in the trough between
each echo, and they were wired up by the mixture of
fatigue, cold, and the first good rest they'd got, and by
the life of the day they had just passed, and by the
clean in them free of mixed shit, and lying without a
gun or knife which was like traveling naked at night
now weaponless in near unmarked mountains watching wolf and griz, mother caribou, the cranes never
forget their hearts starting to beat at the mystery sound
of a thousand cranes' wings near enough to lift your
heart out of your body, make it fly after. So they
breathing hard with all of this, lying next to each other
like two rods getting charged with magnetism in electric coils, the ante going up and up under that blanket,
and in the next half hour as they lay there saying not a
word in an intensity of hung suspension, like purga-
tory so near they are to reaching across, fingers poised,
hands up, throats near to gorging with heartbeat, there
like that over the next half hour the Arctic lights
began, Aurora Borealis was out like she had not been
out any night in September this trip and looked to
begin above their feet across the pond, North of them
in a corona of red and electric green wash and glow
colors rippling like a piece of silk and spikes of light
radiating up like searchlights, diamond spikes from the
crown of the corona going two hundred miles up verti-
cally into the sky while rays and bands, curtains of
light, draperies rustled, pulses of color went up into

handwritten: honosdcialits

the dark, something agitated in the bend of the night, and a crackling sound like agitation of sparks run over a run of silk, some light was alive and spoke to them.

"What cause that?" said Tex.

"Don't know."

"Sunspots."

"Yeah, sunspots."

"Magnetic disturbance?"

"Yeah."

Silence. And they each are living half out of their minds. For the lights were talking to them, and they were going with it, near to, the lights were saying that there was something up here, and it was really here, yeah God was here, and He was real and no man was He, but a beast, some beast of a giant jaw and cavernous mouth with a full cave's breath and fangs, and secret call: come to me. They could almost have got up and walked across the pond and into the north without their boots, going up to disappear and die and join that great beast. In the field of all such desire D.J. raised his hand to put it square on Tex's cock and squeeze and just before he did the Northern lights shifted on that moment and a coil of sound went off in the night like a blowout in some circuit fuse of the structure of the dark and D.J. who had never put a hand on Tex for secret fear that Tex was strong enough to turn him around and brand him up his ass, sheer hell for a noble Texan but he, D.J., was beloved son of perfume on the poo Halleloo and her sweet ass was his sweet ass and so temptation made him weak at the root of his balls and he always swelled to be muscle hard around Tex so that Indian could never get it up his ass nor no man living, and vibrations coming off Tex tonight like he giving up the secret of why he never tried to bugger old D.J., Tex who'd bugger any punk, cause asshole is harder to enter than cunt and so reserved for the special tool but Tex, who never sucked a dick and never let no one near him not even to touch, could bugger all but was never ripe to try for D.J.'s dangerous hard-ass soft mother's cherry although secret unvoiced almost unknown panic for attempting such entrance had him nipped in the groin with a claw, but it came out in the night some tension of waves of unspoken confession from Tex to D.J. that Tex Hyde he of the fearless Eenyen blood was finally afraid to prong D.J., because D.J. once become a bitch would kill him, and D.J. breathing that in by the wide-awake of the dark with Aurora Borealis jumping to the beat of his heart knew he could make a try to prong Tex tonight, there was a chance to get in and steal the iron from Texas' ass and put it in his own and he was hard as a hammer at the thought and ready to give off sparks and Tex was ready to fight him to death, yeah, now it was there, murder between them under all friendship, for God was a beast, not a man, and God said, "Go out and kill—fulfill my will, go and kill," and they hung there each of them on the knife of the divide in all conflict of lust to own the other yet in fear of being killed by the other and as the hour went by and the lights shifted, something in the radiance of the North went into them, and owned their fear, some communion of telepathies and new powers, and they were twins, never to be near as lovers again, but killer brothers, owned by something, prince of darkness, lord of light, they did not know; they just knew telepathy was on them, they had been touched forever by the North and each bit a drop of blood from his own finger and touched them across and met, blood to blood, while the lights pulsated and glow of Arctic night was on the snow, and the deep beast whispering Fulfill my will, go forth and kill, and they left an hour later in the dark to go back to camp and knew on the way each mood of emotion building in Rusty and Big Luke and Ollie and M. A. Bill and Pete and their faces were etched just as they had foreseen them and the older men's voices were filled with the same specific mix of mixed old shit which they had heard before in the telepathic vaults of their new Brooks Range electrified mind.

★

———————————

TERMINAL INTRO BEEP
AND OUT

———————————

★

A ring of vengeance like a pitch of the Saracen's sword
on the quiver (what a movie was that, madame!) rings
out of the air as if all the woe and shit and parsimony
and genuine greed of all those fucking English, Irish,
Scotch and European weeds, transplanted to North
America, that sad deep sweet beauteous mystery land
of purple forests, and pink rock, and blue water, Indian haunts from Maine to the shore of Californ, all
gutted, shit on, used and blasted, man, cause a weed
thrives on a cesspool, piss is its nectar, shit all ambrosia,

and those messages at night—oh, God, let me hump the boss' daughter, let me make it, God, all going up through the M.E.F. cutting the night air, giving a singe to the dream field, all the United Greedies of America humping up that old rhythm, turning the dynamo around, generating, just cut through that magnetism and go, boy, and God got to give it to the Greedies, cause get a man greedy enough and he got the guts to go—go, go, Gutsy Hyde—so the Devil feeding them from one side and God having to juice man from the other, and whoa, whoa, but no, it will not slow, and these messages zoom across the lands, M.E.F. on call, at night—check on this, idiot expert technologue!—the ionization layer rises, the interference is less, the radio messages go further, zoom, zoom, zoom, like pneumatic tubes going back to the lap of Hiram Hardon, President and Head of Head's Dept. Store right up there, Endicott Mountains, Brooks Range, and an hour before sunrise as all those North America shit heads stir in their sleep, digesting the messages they sent out and got back, beginning to smog the predawning air with their psychic glug, glut and exudations, not to mention all the funeral parlors cooling out in the premature morn from the M.E.F. all through the night screams and wails of corpses exhumed, excavated, flushed, sponged, spiced, finger-fucked, flayed, sewn, pushed, cut and shoved, not to mention sliced loose from their organs and petrified man in embalming juice—every undertaker worth his junked-out gunk has a secret

formula—formaldehyde, do not relinquish your secret
ceremonies, your treasure chests, your Paris gardens
where the vestal virgins partouse in your juice, no, sir,
never forget the living, the dead, and the just dead are
fighting up all those square root of minus one bands in
the M.E.F. mystery kc frequently kill your cycles, and
as morning comes on, one hour before dawn, they are
scheming in their sleep, getting practical, getting ready
to get up, yawn, cough, fart, shoot a little piss, just gen-
erally fuck up that M.E.F. band, and so, friends, the
ionization layer (first cousin to static in telepathic af-
fairs) comes down again like a cloud, and intercranial
communication is muffled, no mean matter, cause at
Brooks Range, on the edge of the great snow-white
parabolic reflector, sitting in the silent resonant electric
hum of the still, there is a rub in the air like your hair
on edge or coitus all interruptus with electric coils of
gas in your bowel, pain in your balls, and hate in your
ding, yes, discomfort as the ionization layer settles back
and the hills is full of static charge. And when the shit
was over in the Moe Henry and Obungekat Safari
Group bunkhouse on Dolly Ding Bat Lake and the ice
pinnacles of the Brooks Range was murmuring the
word from ice shield to parabolic vale, "m.e.f., m.e.f.,
roger and out, it's morning, come in, e.m.f.," why,
Rusty and Luke and the guides and boys and packers
and medium assholes all got into the planes to go on
back to Fairbanks and led the way into the new life
smack right up here two years later in my conscious-

ness, D.J. here at this grope dinner in the Dallas ass manse, given in my honor, D.J., I thank you, because tomorrow Tex and me, we're off to see the wizard in Vietnam. Unless, that is, I'm a black-ass cripple Spade and sending from Harlem. You never know. You never know what vision has been humping you through the night. So, ass-head America contemplate your butt. Which D.J. white or black could possibly be worse of a genius if Harlem or Dallas is guiding the other, and who knows which? This is D.J., Disc Jockey to America turning off. Vietnam, hot damn.